The Forgotten Gift

Dora Leigh

BLACK ROSE
writing™

First printing

ISBN: 978-1-61296-527-7

PUBLISHED BY BLACK ROSE WRITING

www.blackrosewriting.com

Printed in the United States of America

Suggested retail price $15.95

The Forgotten Gift is printed in Book Antiqua

This book is dedicated to my daughters, Sharon and Sheila – I could not have done it without you.

Special thanks to Reagan Rothe and Black Rose Writing for publishing this story so that others might benefit from my experience.

The Forgotten Gift

PROLOGUE

MARCH 1997

Claire Breen's gray Lexus whipped into the front parking lot of the *Old Harbor Inn* on the Southern Indiana side of the Ohio River. The inn was indeed old, the wooden structure gray and weather-beaten from more than thirty years at a waterfront residence. Claire had driven the half hour route along I-65 to Highway 56 over from Louisville, Kentucky, her hometown just across the river. She grabbed an empty parking spot among the lunch crowd and hurried into the restaurant.

Inside the nautical-themed dining room life preservers, rusted anchors and tangled fishnet clung to the walls. A long row of floor-to-ceiling windows offered a sunny picture-perfect view of the rambling, silver river and snow-laden woods. Men and women both turned from the rustic scenery and hushed conversation to assess the latest arrival as she followed the host to a window table. She carried a small purse and an elegant bronze gift bag.

At age 33, Claire Breen, in a designer business suit, was still the dazzling, leggy blonde with a face and body created for envy. She pampered her beautiful self with a first-rate management of time and care that only the rich and successful know how to do properly. From an ingenious expression that she expertly worked to her advantage, Claire's penetrating blue eyes took in and dismissed the dining crowd in one compelling glance. She spotted the man seated at a table before the far windows, and a glorious smile lit her face.

Les Connelly was 37 years old and even better to look at as he neared 40. He had the distinctive features of the aristocrat, with brown hair barely going gray, dark blue eyes that saw everything and assessed it accurately, and an easy, you-can-trust-me smile that did wonders for his career. His tailored business suit perfectly fit the six-foot-two, lean body he kept in top shape through a routine exercise program. Les stood as Claire and their elder host approached. The man pulled out a chair for her across the table. She sat down with a nod of thanks to him and laid her purse and gift bag on the chair beside her. Behind them, through the high windows, a long barge towed a freight vessel downstream at a snail's pace.

"What a gorgeous afternoon, Amos," Les said while their host placed menus before them. "Still a bit chilly though."

"It sure is that, Mr. C. Best time of the year 'round here."

Amos left them, and Claire ignored her menu. She said, "I didn't see your car in the parking lot. I thought you weren't here yet."

"I'm having new tires put on," Les replied. "They gave me a loaner."

An hour later, a pretty young woman removed their empty dishes from the table while they finished the last of their white wine.

"Thank you, Marcie," Les said.

The server looked from Les to Claire. "Do either one of you want to see the dessert menu today?"

Les deferred to Claire with a polite glance. "Not today, Marcie. Thank you," she said.

As Marcie left the table, Claire reached for the gift bag that she'd placed in the chair next to her when she'd first sat down. She grinned at her companion.

"I brought you a present."

Les looked surprised. "That was thoughtful of you."

Claire placed the bag on the table in front of him. He didn't move to take it, just looked at it as if he didn't know what was expected of him.

She said, "Well, go on, open it."

"I didn't bring you anything."

She laughed. "Will you open it already!"

Les heaved an enormous sigh and reached for the bronze bag. He pulled out the silvery tissue paper crumpled on top and tossed it aside. He lifted out the gift and stared at it for the longest time. She watched him, her smile turning into a frown.

"You don't like it."

Les looked up at her. "I like it, yes, but...I'm not sure. What am I supposed to do with it, Claire? I—"

He stopped. What he saw in her face now was almost too much. Her love for him. So strong. So real. So...overwhelming. He couldn't refuse her gesture. Even though he took such a risk in accepting the gift. But he couldn't hurt her feelings by refusing. No, he couldn't do that. He wouldn't do that. No. He loved her too much. He'd just have to find a safe place to keep her gift hidden from his wife.

"Okay, Claire. Sure. And thank you."

Les reached for her hand across the table and smiled. His smile melted her heart. She squeezed his fingers. "I do love you, Les. I love you so much."

He smiled again. "I know. I love you too."

Beneath the table, she slipped off one of her high heels and rubbed his leg up and down through his dress pants.

He watched her with increasing desire.

She grinned again, provocatively. "So what's on the agenda for this afternoon?"

CHAPTER 1

With a population of one million plus, Louisville is the largest city in the commonwealth of Kentucky. Discovered by George Rogers Clark and named for Louis XVI of France, it began as a portage site in 1778, but Louisville is best known as the location of the world-renown Kentucky Derby. Held at famed Churchill Downs racetrack, the Derby is the first of three annual races that make up the Triple Crown of thoroughbred racing. (Lexington, Kentucky is the thoroughbred racehorse capital of the world.) The Kentucky Derby Festival, held in Louisville, is the biggest festival in the United States. If the performing arts happen to be your scene, the city's superb offerings in the downtown area are well-known and highly-regarded. Three of Kentucky's six Fortune 500 companies take care of business in Louisville. The city's architecture blends the old and the new, with the largest number of Victorian homes in the country located in an area known as Old Louisville. Heart surgery? Hand surgery? Cancer treatment? Louisville is one of the major healthcare and medical science centers in the U.S.

OCTOBER 2014

In Louisville's affluent East End suburb, old and new money prospered together - shops, offices, restaurants, and golf courses mingled among residential communities with parks of lofty trees, small lakes, and flowers bursting with fall colors. The antebellum style Grand Oaks Country Club nestled in a lush setting off Brownsboro Road. The patio garden was decorated in a Halloween theme, and a private party developed through the early evening. The breeze was soft and warm. Stars twinkled around a crescent moon. A popular local band played old favorites for Dana and Les Connelly and their formally-attired guests—three middle-aged-plus couples, two younger couples, and three middle-aged-plus singles. Claire Breen was among the singles, a mature woman of 50 now, but still a stunning one nonetheless, which was obvious in the revealing cut of her gown. Les, 54 now, looked not much older than he did seventeen years ago at his rendezvous with Claire at the *Old Harbor Inn*, except perhaps for the gray in his hair.

Dana Connelly, at 52, was a classic beauty. At five-foot-six, she was still slender and lovely as ever with dark brown eyes and auburn hair worn in a smooth, blunt cut with highlights covering the gray. Her intelligence and kindness showed in her face, and there was just enough humor in her personality to keep her from taking herself too seriously. She wore a designer evening gown that was elegant in its simplicity.

"You think the party's okay?" Dana asked her husband as they danced. "You're glad we did it?"

"Yes, sweetheart. I just…I wish we…we could've waited another fifteen or twenty years."

"I know, Les. I know."

"I'm not ready to retire. But when you don't have a choice anymore...I should say a few words later, shouldn't I?"

"We worked on your speech yesterday, remember? It's in

your pocket."

"No, Dana, I don't remember," he said bitterly. "That's just the point, though, isn't it? *I don't remember.*"

"Oh, Les, I'm *so* sorry."

He drew her closer for a hug. He kissed her cheek. "No, *I'm* sorry. I don't mean to take what's happened to me out on you."

Later, Dana and Les stood near the bar, drinks in hand. He alternately watched everyone and no one, his mind in and out of the moment. She noticed Claire and her dancing partner, Richard Starnes, handsome, in his fifties, and in his element going around with such a lovely woman.

Dana said, "Les, I've always wondered why Claire's never found anyone. Do you think she and Rich might get together now that his divorce is final?"

Les pretended to study the dancing pair across the patio. "No, I don't think that will happen."

"You sound so sure. Why not?"

"Why not? Well…I…I think it would've happened by now, if it was going to."

"But he was married. Happily, I thought."

"Well, yes, but you know that—" he slammed to a stop. How did he get into this conversation? And with his wife of all people? And how did he get out of it?

"So… sweetheart, should I say a few words now? What am I going to say? I didn't write a speech—"

"Your speech is in your pocket, Les. We wrote it together yesterday."

"We did?" He fumbled in his jacket's outer pockets.

"No," Dana said, "it's in your inside pocket."

Les reached into his open jacket and pulled out a folded paper. "I should just look it over again, shouldn't I? Did I bring my glasses?"

He groped through his pockets again and watched as Pete Myers, big, fifties, African American, roamed around snapping pictures among the guests. Pete reached Dana and Les near the bar and paused as Les gave up trying to find his glasses. He slipped the folded speech back in his pocket.

Holding onto his camera, Pete said, "Les, I sure hate adding your retirement party pictures to the office album."

"How big is the album now, Pete, after almost thirty years?" Dana asked as Claire and Richard danced over to them.

"You'll have to ask Claire that one. She's our official keeper of the album."

Dana asked her question of Claire when she and Richard paused at the bar to order drinks. After taking care of that, while the band swung into a lively number, Claire reminisced about her eighteen years with one of Louisville's most prestigious law firms: how Les and Pete had given her the opportunity to prove herself and how she hoped—believed—that she hadn't disappointed them. Claire focused on Les then, and if she thought he had an opening now to chime in with a supporting comment, he evidently didn't agree. Instead, he finished his drink, sat the empty glass on the bar and reached for his wife's hand.

"If you'll excuse us, Claire, Rich, I think I'm suddenly starving."

Even though this was partly true, Les *was* hungry; however, what he actually had in mind was separating his wife and his lover. A three-way conversation here was absolutely beyond his ability to finesse these days.

Dana and Les loaded their plates at the lavish buffet across the patio as an attendant replenished the array of food choices. They carried them over to the formal dining table set up beneath the trees. The long table filled up quickly, sixteen people enjoying the meal together. Suddenly, Les turned to his wife.

"Dana, sweetheart, have I told you how gorgeous you look tonight?"

She smiled. "Yes, but you may tell me again."

They exchanged intimate looks, and down the table Claire ignored them and focused on her sparsely-filled plate with all the gusto of a famished waif.

Guests came and went from the buffet until they began pushing back from the table, more than sated. Les gazed around, taking note.

"I should probably say a few words now, shouldn't I, Dana? Something official about why I'm retiring so early. I mean everybody knows. I messed up in court, didn't I? More than once, I…I think."

"That's when you decided it was time to retire."

"But what am I going to say now? I don't have a speech. Not anything official."

"Honey, your speech is in your inside pock—" She sighed, wearily. Never mind. "You know, why don't you just wing it? Say whatever's in your heart."

Les stared at her, his expression as blank as an empty computer screen. At last, he rose from his chair and conversations dropped off. A minute passed while he gazed around at all of them. They gazed back with caring and respect. He seemed at a loss for how he should begin. The silence settled over them and threatened to become awkward as Les found himself overcome with emotion. Finally, he managed to pull himself together and organize his thoughts.

"I want to thank everyone for coming tonight. You don't know how much this party means to me. Dana, for all the planning. And each one of you for showing up." Soft laughter swept around the table. "I didn't intend to even consider retirement for another decade at least. Maybe two. But—" He stopped. His feelings threatened to erupt again. He fought them down with effort. "Life...life has a way of...of changing the plan sometimes."

Les paused. He grappled with more emotion that he couldn't stop this time, turning to Dana for assurance. She smiled warmly up at him and that seemed to be enough to anchor him once more. He winked at her and she laughed. The tension that had been growing around the table dispersed and everybody relaxed. Les gave his brief speech for his colleagues—fellow attorneys and their legal assistants, including all the spouses or significant others. At the conclusion, he reached down for his wine glass and lifted it high, smiling.

"Here's to the best law firm in the city of Louisville!"

Cheers rose from the group, and Les set his glass down on the table. Then his face went blank again.

"Oh, now what was I going to say?" He turned helplessly to his wife. "Dana, sweetheart?"

"You aren't just my colleagues..." she prompted.

"Oh, yes. You aren't just my colleagues at Breen, Connelly, Jansen...Meyers...Starnes...and Woodall. There! That's all of us, right? That's how I remember all the partners now—alphabetically. And then there's our legal assistants— Chirelle, Kyle, and Rosa—without whose expert help none of the partners could function."

"Hear! Hear!" Chanted all the partners, simultaneously. And afterwards, Les looked completely lost once more. His eyes found Dana again.

"What else was I going to say, sweetheart?"

"You were going to explain what's wrong—"

Les cut her off. "But what is it exactly? I can't…I don't…know how..." He stopped, lost yet again. He looked at his wife, frustrated.

She stood beside him, coming to the rescue. She slipped her hand in his and looked around at their friends, explaining that Les was in early-stage dementia. Which caused, among other things, short-term memory loss. This meant that he could no longer make new memories. He could recall events from twenty years past, but couldn't remember what he did ten minutes ago.

"But I haven't forgotten everything yet," Les interjected. "I still remember how to play golf!"

Everyone laughed with him, and then Pete stood up.

"I think it's written somewhere that you can forget your name, your age, your job, even your wife's birthday, but God forbids a man to forget how to play golf!"

The table of friends and coworkers broke up laughing at this bit of nonsense as Claire came to her feet and waited for the fun to subside.

"The last thing we want you to do is leave us, Les," she said, "but we understand why you made this decision."

The guests joined Claire, raising their glasses in a toast to Les that seemed to embarrass him in its sincerity. How grateful he was for these friends!

Later, Dana strolled around the country club grounds with Pete and his wife, Gloria, tallish, in her fifties, and African American like her husband. The old trees on the property shed red and gold and brown leaves along their meandering path. The setting sun edged below the distant horizon.

"Dementia is the general term," Dana said, "for a decline in mental ability severe enough to interfere with daily life. It can occur in any phase of adulthood, but the onset usually strikes among the elderly population. It's rare among people our age."

"They know what causes dementia now, don't they?" asked Gloria.

"They know what causes it, Gloria—death of nerve cells in the brain. Or the loss of communication among the cells. From plaque deposits. But they don't know *why*. The brain is so complex. Researchers haven't put all the puzzle pieces together yet."

Pete said, "I read somewhere that they also believe now that genes might play a role in causing dementia."

"They also think that dementia develops over a long period of time," Dana added, "and can be influenced by lifestyle factors."

"What kind of factors?" Gloria asked.

"Everything from medical conditions to eating and sleeping habits to mental, physical and social activity."

"So what's the prognosis for Les?" Pete asked.

"Dementia eventually affects all the cognitive area—memory, focus, attention, communication and language. It even affects reasoning and judgment. And sometimes alters visual perception."

Gloria said, "What's the treatment program?"

"There are a couple of drugs that delay dementia progression. Also, mental stimulation and social interaction helps. Within a routine and simplified environment."

"So basically," Pete said, "Les takes his meds, challenges his mind, and physically stays inside his comfort zone."

"You got it, Pete."

CHAPTER 2

The Connelly's lived in a two-story house designed in the English Tudor style and built on a picture-pretty landscape of towering old trees in Grand Oaks Village, a cozy community in the East End of Louisville. Grinning jack o'lanterns sat out front in keeping with the late October Halloween theme. Though Les had always been happy and proud that he could provide his family—Dana and their son and daughter twins—with the best things that life had to offer, he had never appreciated being called "one of those upper-crust guys." An ancient term anyway, and "upper" made him think of snobbish, which he definitely was not. He had specialized in criminal law, meaning he had seen it all, and a felony courtroom was not the place for arrogance. As for "crust," that reminded him of a hard surface, something unyielding. Les could be a tough man, he had to be in his chosen field, but he wasn't a hard one. Call him an aging yuppie if you want to, but spare him your inglorious judgments. Family and friends knew he was actually just an old softie.

In the master bathroom on the second floor, Dana wore a sheer nightgown and creamed her face at the mirror over the vanity. Les strolled in dressed down to his boxers and a T-shirt.

At the sink beside his wife, he took out his toothbrush.

"The party went well tonight, didn't it? Did I make a speech?"

"Mmm," Dana replied.

"Does that mean yes?"

She wiped cream off her hands with a face towel and patted his arm, forestalling his next question. "It means you did fine."

The master bedroom was richly decorated in a traditional furniture style with vintage accents and had an adjoining sitting room with French doors to the balcony stretching across the back of the house. Wearing glasses, Dana was reading in bed when Les came in from the bathroom and joined her beneath the covers. He cuddled next to her, interrupting her, but she didn't object. She welcomed what he had in mind. One of the richest blessings of their union was their sex life. Still active after twenty-five years together. Still exciting. Still romantic. Because they'd never taken it for granted.

"I love the way you smell, sweetheart," he said. "What is it when we go to bed?"

Dana slid off her glasses and laid them and her book on the bedside table. "My night cream."

"You're my night dream."

She smiled. Les had been telling her that since their honeymoon, and she never tired of hearing it. "I love you too, honey."

They kissed and she reached over, turning off the lamp. They lay together in an affectionate embrace.

"I said a few words at the party, didn't I, sweetheart?"

"Yes."

He drew her closer. "How many times have I asked you this?"

"It doesn't matter. What's so good is that you remember

your party."

Suddenly he sounded dejected. "My *retirement* party."

She squeezed his hand. "Don't go there. Let's fool around a little bit instead."

"Let's fool around a whole lot. I sure haven't forgotten how to do that."

Dana smiled and they kissed again.

* * *

The fitness room was located on the lower level of the Connelly's home. The next morning, dressed in old sweats, Les jogged on the treadmill before a glass wall. He wore headphones, listening to a favorite classical piece. He watched the rain fall steadily and distort the view of shedding trees on the lawn. Across the room Dana, in a jogging suit, tackled the stationary bike, finally slowing to a stop as her husband finished his workout and removed his headphones.

She said, "Would today be a good day to go over and clean out your office? With no one in on Sunday. Maybe no one will be there. It might be easier for you to pack up. Especially if I'm with you. What do you think?"

"Sure. Today's okay. But cleaning out my office is going to be hard no matter when I do it. But you don't have to go. I'm...I'm a big boy, I can handle it by myself, sweetheart."

"I know you can do it, honey, but..."

He hopped off the treadmill. "But what?"

Dana stared at him. He didn't remember, he *couldn't* remember now, even though they'd been through this routine how many times?

"But what, Dana?"

She stared at him some more, but Les was quick, still quick.

He had hardly lost all of his reasoning skills at once. He fled past her like a man running for his life and in a way he was. He took the steps two at time up to the main level. She slid off the exercise bike and followed him more slowly. She sighed, dreading another Audi ordeal.

At the doorway to the garage, in the short hall between the kitchen and the half bath, Les stood with the door pushed open. He gazed into the three-car area at his workbench with tools scattered around, an old refrigerator, a leaf blower, and a riding lawn mower. There was only one vehicle in there, Dana's silver Volvo SUV. She came up behind him and gently hugged his back.

He said, "Where's my car?"

She sighed again, dramatically. "We sold it, Les."

Frustrated, angry suddenly, he shouted at her. "Why did we sell it?"

She hugged him tighter. "Les— "

"Why did we sell my Audi? You know I love that car."

Dana wished for a way to spare him from the truth. Again. But how could she?

"Because you don't drive anymore. You forget now…you forget directions and…well…well…"

"Well what?" When she didn't answer, he whirled around and accidentally sent her flying backwards. "What, Dana? What? Tell me!"

Les helped her regain her balance. "Sometimes you…well…you get…lost."

Les stared at his wife while he gave that some thought. Gradually, the frustration and anger dissipated until it left him. Left him dejected. "I am lost, Dana," he said in an empty voice. "I am lost."

* * *

Dana drove her SUV through Grand Oaks Village and along Brownsboro Road past the old post office, the new shopping plaza, and the antiquated courthouse square. Les slumped in the passenger's seat and stared out at the suburban scenery, watching Halloween-decorated stores and restaurants go by. The rain had ended and the sun was out in all its splendid glory. Everything looked scrubbed and bright in the clear sky. She had offered to let him drive them to their destination, but he had declined. If he needed a babysitter to do the job, then he'd rather not do it, Les had said. But he did apologize to her for his outburst, and she forgave him. She understood that he could hardly be held accountable for his debilitating mental condition. Dementia struck where it would, without regard for intelligence or a lack thereof.

Dana swung off into the side parking lot of the Oaks office building and slid into a spot near the front doors. In the lobby they rode the elevator to the 4th floor, got off and walked the short distance to a glass door embossed with six names—CONNELLY, MEYERS, BREEN, WOODALL, JANSEN and STARNES. ATTORNEYS AT LAW was printed below the six names. Les took out his keys and opened the door. He trailed his wife into the law office.

In his corner office with a broad window wall above a small park, Les sat at the desk cleaning out a drawer into a box, while Dana took law books down from the wall shelves and packed them into boxes.

"I was right," he said, "this is the hardest thing I've ever had to do. Remember when we started out here? Just Pete and me. And you were our legal secretary."

"Until we were ready to have kids. About two years later.

Then after Gwen and Graham were born, I went part-time."

"Until you chose to be a full-time mom."

"Can you remember when we met?'

"Yes, I can. Like it was yesterday."

FEBRUARY 1980

The University of Louisville campus on Third Street just west of Eastern Parkway and I-65 wasn't far from the city's downtown area. *Grounded*, the neighborhood coffee shop around the corner was a favorite student hangout. Snow came down hard as Les strode to the door wearing jeans and a red U of L jacket. Dana hurried up from the opposite direction in her college jacket and jeans. They arrived at the same time and their eyes met. For an instant neither one could look away.

He smiled. *Wow! My dream come true.*

She smiled. *Wow! The man of my dreams.*

Les pushed the door open, still smiling like a fool. "After you."

"Thank you," Dana said, and he followed her inside.

The coffee shop tables were crowded with students doing homework and letting their coffees grow cold. At the serving counter, Dana and Les ordered the house drink and stood there doing a lot more gazing at each other than they did sipping their steaming coffees. Who would break the magic spell?

"I just transferred here from junior college," she said. "Two years was all I planned to do. Then I decided to go for four."

"What will you do with your four?" he asked.

"I want to be a legal assistant in some great law firm."

"That's perfect. Because I'm going on to law school, and then open my own great law office."

"Don't forget to pass the Bar exam while you're at it."

"I'm going to ace the Bar," he replied, not with arrogance, but with confidence. "But I'll have to work for somebody else for a few years. Until I can afford to go out on my own. So why don't you want to go to law school?"

"I think I have the intelligence, but I'm better as a back-up person. I want to use my skills and education behind the scenes. Great lawyers need great support, right?"

Les smiled some more and took Dana's nearly full coffee cup and placed it on the counter with his. He reached for her hand and started for the door. When she tugged her hand from his, he glanced back.

"Wait a minute," she said. "We shouldn't leave our cups sitting here in the way."

"You're right. What was I thinking?" He'd never be able to think straight again in the presence of this wonderful, beautiful creature.

He grabbed both coffee cups and dashed over to the trash bin, carefully depositing them inside. He came back and took her hand again and they walked to the door. They stepped out into the falling snow and he said, "Let's dance."

She gaped at him. "Dance? Are you crazy? It's freezing out here. Besides, we don't have any music."

Les gently took her in his arms. "We'll make our own music."

They slow-danced in the falling snow while he hummed to her in a commanding, fluid baritone created for the courtroom. Up and down the sidewalk they flowed and swayed, oblivious of cars passing by, horns honking encouragement. People strolled along, nodding their approval. And on they danced as he sang in her ear and she smiled, and both of them somehow knew that this was it, that together they would last forever.

OCTOBER 2014

In his corner office Les carried over a packed box from his desk and set it by the open door to the hall before going back for another one.

"I didn't realize how much junk I'd accumulated over the years," he said. "Like most people, I guess."

Dana glanced up from the bookcase wall where she loaded his law books into boxes. "You can go through those boxes at home. That'll keep you occupied for a while. And then some."

"Going through boxes is *not* my idea of how to transition from full-time employment to…to all-the-time retirement."

"Well, no, of course not."

"There has to be a better way."

"You'll think of something…Honey, I need one more box over here."

"Okay. Sure. I'll get it from the storage room."

Les took off and Dana finished the box she was filling up. As she lifted another book from the shelf, a blue envelope with a greeting card inside slid from between the pages and landed on the carpet at her feet. She laid the book in a box and retrieved the envelope. Les's first name was written in a neat, feminine style on the front, but it wasn't in her handwriting. Curious, she hesitated to look inside the envelope. It was addressed to her husband, after all.

Finally, her desire to know won out over her sense of propriety and she removed the blue and white card and stared, frozen in shock at the large letters printed across the front in a fancy calligraphy: HAPPY ANNIVERSARY TO THE ONE I LOVE. Reaching for her purse on the nearby club chair, Dana pulled out her reading glasses, slipped them on and opened the card. She skipped over the inside verse down to the signature at the bottom: ALL MY LOVE, CLAIRE. She sucked in a paralyzing breath and stared in disbelief at the signature. She couldn't stop staring at it.

At last, she turned her eyes to the handwritten note on the left side of the card: *I hope the gift that I gave you seventeen years ago, foolish though it might have been, still keeps us close to your heart when we're not together. I love you more than you will ever know, Claire.* Below the note, Claire had penned the date—*July 2014.*

Too stunned now to even move—Dana could barely breathe—she studied the card until Les's voice coming from down the hall penetrated her shock. His voice grew louder as he approached.

"Have I ever told you how glad I am that you're the tax law expert around here?" he asked. "Because I never did like that stuff."

Quickly, Dana slid Claire's anniversary card back into the envelope and tucked it into her purse. She jerked off her glasses and dropped them inside too. She looked up when Les walked in with an empty box in his hands and Claire at his side. She wore crisp jeans and a checked shirt, and looked as lovely as she did in a formal gown. They paused, watching Dana, who stood there as if she were a statue in the park, unable to think, unable to react, unable to even breathe now.

"Dana, sweetheart, look who's here," Les said, crossing the room to his desk. He sat down the box and smiled.

Claire spoke from the doorway. "Hi, Dana. Great party last night." She checked her watch. "I'll see you guys later. I've got a pain-in-the-you-know-where client due in my office any minute to sign some M & A papers."

Ms. Lovely-As-Ever disappeared down the hallway, and Dana stared at the empty space where Claire had been seconds ago. She took a breath, finally, but her mind still couldn't quite function. All she could think about were Claire's parting words: M & A papers. Mergers and Acquisitions. The words stuck in her brain as if she'd never heard them before. Mergers and Acquisitions...Mergers and Acquisitions...Mergers and...

* * *

Dana pulled out of the parking lot next to the Oaks office building and eased her SUV into the late afternoon traffic. Numb with ongoing shock, she was functioning more or less on auto-pilot now. She drove without really registering anything. Beside her, Les stared glumly out the passenger's window at the passing shop windows. She had managed not to give herself away to him and Claire back at his office, but by this time she wondered how she could fake it for much longer. Unlike them. How could they appear so normal in front of her? Well, why not? They'd had seventeen years of practice. *Seventeen years.* She couldn't get her mind around that length of time. Most of her and Les's married life. Happily married life. Or so she thought.

"I'll come back to the office and visit occasionally," Les was saying. "Maybe I...I can even do some consulting for a while. What do you think, sweetheart?"

Dana didn't even hear him. She slipped through a yellow traffic light in front of the library almost without realizing it. Luckily, traffic wasn't heavy.

"Or am I kidding myself?" he asked.

No reply from his wife and he glanced over at her. "Dana?"

She stopped at the next traffic light as it went red and stared at the thing swinging in the breeze as if she'd never seen one before. Slowly, she turned to Les. Had he said something to her? She stared at him. She stared *through* him. A minute later, after the light changed to green, a horn blared somewhere behind them and her foot hit the gas pedal. They shot forward and she slammed the brakes to keep from rear-ending the car in front of them. The horn on the car directly in back of them blasted.

"Sunday drivers. That must be us today," Les said. "It is Sunday, right?"

When there was yet no comment from his wife, he decided that she had her mind on driving and nothing else. They rode in silence for a few minutes.

"I can keep busy at home," he continued. "There's plenty to do around the place. I hope this warmer weather holds for a while."

She drove on in her auto-pilot daze and didn't respond again.

"Maybe I'll…I'll take over the cooking. Expand my weekend hobby."

Dana's cell phone chirped down in her purse, startling her from her stupor. She fumbled for it and snagged Claire's envelope. She glanced at Les. He looked occupied with the colorful view out his side window of a weekend sale on fall flowers at the local nursery. She located her phone and checked the caller ID before taking the call.

"Hi, Gwen!"

She had to fake the cheery hello. And that pushed her into a whole new wave of depressing thoughts. How could she tell the twins about their dad and Claire? Well, she couldn't, of course. She wouldn't. Not in this lifetime. Not in a hundred lifetimes. They not only loved their father, they idolized him. After all, Les helped God hang the moon, didn't he? That big, handsome dad with the great courtroom voice who loved his family even more than his career. She jerked in a strangled breath.

"Hey, Mom," Gwen said. "I got your message from earlier. So what's on tonight? Food, am I right?"

Gwen Connelly was twenty-two years old, taller than her mom, but as slender as she was. Gwen had brown hair and brown eyes. A senior at the University of Louisville, Gwen wanted to be a pediatrician and planned to go on to the medical school there. She and her brother were born at the same time and resembled each other, but no more than any other pair of siblings. Gwen was a bit of a pixie personality, with a balanced blend of her mom's class and her dad's dignity.

Dana pictured Gwen lounging on the bed in her dorm room wearing red sweats with the U of L logo on the front of the shirt. Her wall space was filled up with newspaper photos and clippings about the Louisville Cardinals, the university's 2013 National Championship basketball team. Most of the pictures were of the team's former captain, Luke Hancock. Now graduated, Luke was the 2013 NCAA Final Four Outstanding Player. In the honored place above her bed, in a glass-enclosed frame, hung Luke's famed #11 red jersey with his autograph. The highlight of her life had been meeting him at a local autograph signing. She especially remembered how much he enjoyed interacting with his fans.

"Mom, did you hear me?" Gwen said into her cell phone. "I got your message. So tell me about tonight?"

"I'm driving right now, honey, and you know I don't drive and talk on the phone at the same time. So let me—"

"I'll keep it short, I promise. So you've got food?"

"The caterers dropped off the leftovers from Dad's party."

"I'll be there. Have you talked to Graham?"

"I left him a message this morning too," Dana said. "I thought—"

Dana stopped. Her emotions had caught up with her without warning. Les and Dana. Les and Claire. Les and Dana and Claire. Oh, how—

"Mom, where did you go?"

She couldn't respond.

"Mom?"

"Oh, I…well, I thought that…since we've got all this…this food…well, I…we…we might as well have our own little get together for…for your dad…just us…I mean the four of us."

"Yeah, sure, Mom. And Graham will bring Leah."

"Oh, I forgot Leah for a minute. Sure, Leah too…Are you bringing a date?"

"Mom! When do I have time to date? So is Dad with you?"

She glanced over at Les. He was still taking in the local scenery out the side window as if he'd never seen it before. She thrust the phone at him.

"Here, Gwen wants to talk to you."

Dana drew up at a four-way stop sign and waited on a passing minivan before turning off Brownsboro Road onto Grand Oaks Parkway. She followed the winding lane divided by a grassy median through their luxurious neighborhood of high-end homes. Amid the pumpkins and scarecrows scattered about, leaves tumbled from the brilliant trees, littering perfect lawns and meandering sidewalks.

"Hi, Gwenie, sweetheart," Les said into the cell phone.

"So, Dad, how was your party?"

"I think your mom said I gave a nice speech…Now, sweetheart, you're in med school, that's right, isn't it?"

"At U of L. Go Cards!"

"What's that about cards?"

"Dad, the Cards, the Louisville Cardinals basketball team."

"Oh, yes, right…Now, Gwenie, are you specializing?"

"Pediatrics."

"What about your brother now? I can't recall. I'm sorry. Did he drop out of college? Yes, he did, I think."

"Graham's still trying to find himself, Dad. He does odd jobs at the marina on River Road. That's where he lives now. On a houseboat with two of his friends."

"Oh, for heaven's sake. Graham's living on a boat?"

* * *

At the Connelly's two-story house, Dana parked her SUV in their attached garage and cut off the motor while the overhead door rolled down.

"Maybe I'm not being fair to Graham," Les said as they got out. "Maybe he really can't find a better job. I understand that he wants to do things on his own without any help from us. Or our friends." He went around behind the SUV and followed her into the house. "But I wish he'd go back to school. That's where he needs to be right now. Without an education, he doesn't have a chance

CHAPTER 3

The Connelly's spacious kitchen of pecan wood cabinets and top-of-the-line appliances had an Italian theme carried out in the wallpaper, countertops, and decorative accents. Les stood at the island counter arranging chicken breasts coated in olive oil in a large casserole dish. At the double sinks, he rinsed and dried his hands before opening a cabinet door on his left. Glassware. He moved to the next door by the fridge. More glassware. He stepped to the right of the sink and opened a door. Dishes. Another door. More dishes. On the adjacent wall he encountered cookware in the cabinets. He strolled over to the back staircase, looking up into the empty second floor hallway.

"Dana, where do we keep the fresh garlic?" he called out. He waited but there was no reply. "Dana, sweetheart, where do we keep the fresh garlic?"

Her voice drifted down from the master suite. "What? Oh. In the vegetable bin."

"Where's the veg—"

She cut him off. "Why?"

"Why? Why what?"

"Why are you looking for the garlic?"

"I'm making that chicken casserole. The kids are coming

over for dinner tonight, right? That's one of their favorites, isn't it?"

Dana appeared up in the hall and with an effort said, "We've got the leftovers from the party, remember? The caterers dropped them off. I put them in the old fridge in the garage. There's way too much food for just us. We don't need any more."

Les nodded and watched his wife disappear back toward the bedroom. He shook his head. He couldn't remember anything these days. He didn't remember the leftovers. He didn't even remember that his own children were coming over. Well, maybe he did recall that. He *was* making the casserole for them. But he just wasn't much good now. Not mentally. In fact, he was fast becoming useless in the brain realm. He didn't go to the office anymore. He didn't drive anymore. What good was he now? He stopped and shrugged. No, he wouldn't go down that road. The road to nowhere. No, he'd get on with the business at hand. Which was what? Oh, yes. The casserole. The chicken casserole. If he could find the fresh garlic. Now where was that veggie bin?

* * *

Logs blazed in the outdoor fireplace on the terrace behind the house. Autumn flowers bloomed around the back lawn, where old trees dropped their bright leaves on the grass. The evening sky darkened and stars glimmered into view. Lanterns hanging from the tree limbs lit up the terrace. At a big, round table, Dana and Les ate gourmet leftovers and chicken casserole with Gwen and Graham and his girlfriend Leah Mullins. Twenty-two-year-old Graham was tall and as good to look at as his dad was. He had his old man's dark hair—minus the gray—and his mom's brown eyes. And unlike his lively sister, he was as laid back as a vacationer at the beach. Leah, at twenty-one, was petite and pretty, with long dark-blond hair and flashing blue eyes. Gwen still had on her U of L sweats. Graham and Leah wore jeans and long-sleeve T-shirts with the words RIVER ROAD LANDING brushed across the front. Les and the kids chatted casually as they ate while Dana played with her food. Silent. Lost in her own thoughts. Gwen finally picked up on her mom's unusual behavior and kept glancing over at her with concerned looks.

The breakfast bay and the hearth room spread across the rear of the Connelly's house in an open floor plan with the kitchen. The décor was a traditional and vintage blend with the kitchen's Italian accents. Gwen and Leah carried in dishes from the terrace via the French doors in the breakfast area. In the kitchen they loaded the dishwasher while Dana filled plastic containers with the remaining leftovers. She was on auto-pilot still, going through the motions only because she had to. When would the shock wear off? In the hearth room, Les started logs in the fireplace and Graham relaxed on the sofa aiming the remote at the HDTV. He was surfing channels when Leah joined him a few minutes later. They hugged and kissed before she deftly relieved him of the remote control and resolved his dilemma of what to watch with a U of L football game in winning progress.

Leah settled in next to him on the sofa. "Your mom said to take the rest of the food to the boat."

"Great! Thanks, Mom!"

No reply from Dana as she bagged the food containers at the counter. Gwen started the dishwasher and watched her mother.

"Are you okay?" When Dana didn't answer, Gwen tried again. "Is something wrong, Mom? Mom?" Nothing, so Gwen stepped around and got in her mother's face. "Are you okay?"

Obviously not.

Dana jerked to attention. "I'm sorry, honey. What did you say?"

"What's wrong with you?"

"Oh…I'm…I'm just tired."

Suddenly, Dana had to struggle with unexpected tears. What was this? She wasn't a crier. She won the battle and faked a smile. But she stretched it a little too big.

"You're not telling me something," Gwen said.

Dana shook her head. Which was the wrong thing to do. The gesture seemed to loosen more tears, and this time she couldn't hold them back. One by one they trickled down her cheeks.

Over in the hearth room, logs blazed in the fireplace and Les had joined Graham and Leah in cheering their favorite football team to victory, unaware of the tangled emotions in the kitchen. A commercial came on and interrupted the game. Relaxed in a recliner, Les looked over at his son.

"Are you working, son?"

"Yeah, Dad, at River Road Landing."

"I guess I knew that. You're living there, right?"

Graham reached for Leah's hand and they entwined fingers. "On a houseboat with Dallas and Juno, my friends from high school. I told you."

Over in the kitchen, Gwen hugged her mom as the tears flowed now. Dana simply couldn't control them. The shock had finally worn off.

"I'm not leaving until you tell me what's wrong," Gwen said. "You never cry."

Dana stepped around her daughter and grabbed a tea towel lying on the center island. She dabbed at her face and glanced into the hearth room. "I can't talk now."

Gwen's eyes followed her mother's. "Tomorrow then. After

my morning classes. We can meet for lunch."

"No, honey. I…well…I don't want to talk to you about this."

Gwen looked at her mom as if she'd just taken a bite out of the tea towel. "We're having a cozy family gathering and you're standing in the middle of the kitchen, crying. Something you never do. And you don't want to talk to me about it?"

Dana stared at her daughter.

Gwen said, "This doesn't make sense."

"I can't talk about…I just…I can't."

Over in the hearth room, Leah excused herself during a replay in the ballgame and headed toward the half bath.

Les looked at Graham and said, "I hope you're going to…to finish school, son."

"Everyone's not cut out for college, Dad."

* * *

Later that night, upstairs in the master suite, Les came into the sitting room from the balcony wearing his pajamas and closed the French doors.

"The stars sure are beautiful out there tonight."

Dana was already in bed. She felt numb. She faced the wall away from him and pretended to be asleep. He climbed in next to her and slipped under the covers. Leaning over, he kissed her hair.

"You're my night dream," he whispered.

She tensed. Her eyes flew open. Oblivious, he turned over and was asleep almost immediately. In the moonlight that seeped in around the draperies, she stared at the wall and listened to his soft snoring. Her gaze wandered about the room and landed on a collage of photos grouped on the wall. Gwen and Graham as infants and toddlers. Dana looked at their children and remembered.

* * *

In the hospital room twenty-two years ago, she sat on one side of the bed and Les sat on the other. She held a blue blanket-wrapped newborn and he held a pink blanket-wrapped newborn. They looked over and smiled at each other. Les reached for her hand and held on tightly.

"Now we're complete," he said.

* * *

Dana's thoughts returned to the present, and she closed her eyes. She tried so hard to blink back the tears, but they tumbled out anyway. She who never cried muffled a sob, and Les slept on in untroubled serenity. And she both envied and resented him.

The next morning Dana slept in, buried beneath a mound of blankets. Les entered from the hallway, still in his pajamas, and went directly to the French doors in the sitting area and yanked open the draperies. Sunlight dazzled the suite as he turned to the bed.

He said, "Rise and shine, sleepyhead!" No response from his wife. "Dana? Sweetheart? Breakfast is ready." Silence. "I made your favorite."

He stepped over and tugged off her covers. She roused and dragged them back on. Buried herself deeper. Deeper.

"You know what time it is? No, of course you don't. Breakfast is actually brunch now. So ten more minutes is…is all you get."

He vanished through the door to the hallway. She still didn't move. Seconds ticked by. A full minute. Suddenly, she scrambled from under the blankets and squinted at the clock radio on the bedside table. Eleven-thirty three. She leaped out of bed, almost stumbling over the hem of her nightgown in her haste, and ran for the bathroom.

Twenty minutes later, Dana dashed down the back stairs into the breakfast room dressed in a jogging suit and jacket, taking her keys out of her purse. She slammed to a halt. The table was set with their best linen placemats and their finest bone china around a lovely floral centerpiece. How did Les manage this? Well, the centerpiece always sat there, the china was in plain sight in the hutch in the dining room, and the placemats were in one of the drawers. Give the man some credit. He may be declining now, with good days and bad days. Today had to be a good one. And he was still a lawyer, wasn't he? A trial lawyer to be exact. One of the best as a matter of fact. And they famously—or was it infamously?—didn't miss anything that even remotely entered their environment.

The smell of perking coffee mingled with frying eggs and bacon and baking biscuits. Les stepped over from the kitchen, still in his pajamas, and offered Dana a glass of orange juice. He checked her out carefully. The jacket. The car keys.

"You're going somewhere before breakfast?" He looked broken hearted.

* * *

Dana parked her SUV in an empty spot beside the *Garden Gate* restaurant on Brownsboro Road. She jumped out and rushed around the building to the front door. In the foyer the hostess led her into the dining room where Gwen waited at a table before a wall of windows overlooking the lush Grand Oaks Country Club golf course. Around the walls hung a variety of large paintings abounding in color and depicting garden scenes for which the restaurant was named. Gwen had on jeans and a long-sleeve T-shirt with the words GO LUKE printed across the front. Her U of L jacket hung from the back of her chair. Dana sat down across from Gwen and slid off her jacket and placed it on an empty chair at the table with her purse. Their server brought water glasses at once. They ordered salads and Gwen asked for hot tea. Dana had to have her morning coffee. There was little hope for her before that first cup, but she hadn't taken time to drink it at home. She wondered how many cups it would take to get her through this impossibly anguishing experience. While they waited for their orders, Dana stared out the window at the number of golfers who'd ignored today's chilly weather to play their beloved game. Gwen stared at her mother and wondered what was going on with her.

At last Dana said, "*Garden Gate*. Sounds like the name of a cemetery."

"You *are* in a mood, aren't you? What in the world, Mom?"

Dana stared outside some more. How should she handle this? How? She didn't have the first clue. Nothing in her life up to now had prepared her for this. How did she tell Gwen that her father—

Their server arrived with their drinks and salads, dressings on the side. She checked with her guests that everything was as requested, and then departed quietly and left them to it. Dana, fork in hand, stabbed at the contents of her huge bowl of veggies as if she didn't know where to begin, completely disregarding her dressing on the side.

Gwen observed and said, "You're eating that?"

Dana looked up at her, clearly puzzled. "What?"

"Don't you see them? You hate blue cheese. But you forgot to tell our server to hold the blue cheese crumbles. I should've reminded you."

Dana laid down her fork with a grimace and pushed her salad bowl away. She reached for her coffee mug and blew and sipped. "I didn't even notice the blue cheese."

"Mom, please tell me what's going on."

Miserable, Dana gazed across the table at her daughter.

"Talk to me!"

"I don't think I can, honey. You shouldn't have to— "

She stopped and squeezed her eyes shut against the sudden welling tears. She wiped at them with the back of her hand.

"When did I become such a cry baby?"

Quietly, she blew her nose on the napkin. Gwen gaped, horrified. She glanced around the busy dining room. No one paid them any attention and she relaxed.

"Mom, you just blew your nose on your napkin."

Dana stared at the napkin as if she'd never seen it before. Finally, she folded the thing back on her lap.

Gwen said, "What. Is. Wrong?"

"I don't want to tell you, but I sure don't want anyone else to know. Not even my closest friends. I ran off and left your dad a while ago. All by himself. Eating this terrific breakfast he made. And *I'm* feeling guilty. Why do I feel guilty? I haven't done...He's the one who..."

She went back to her napkin. Wiping. Blotting. Gwen looked on, helplessly.

"This is so humiliating," Dana said at last. "Well, maybe embarrassing is a better word. Why should I be ashamed? And, of course, I could tell Joan. We've been best friends since high school. She'd never say anything to anyone."

"Tell me what you're talking about, Mom, please! Obviously whatever this is, you can't go through it alone."

Dana looked at Gwen for the longest time. Finally, she laid

her napkin aside and dug into her purse on the chair next to her. She pulled out Claire's envelope.

"I helped your dad clean out his office yesterday and found this."

She slid the anniversary card out of the envelope and passed it across the table. Gwen picked it up and read it outside and inside. Twice. Then she lifted her eyes to her Mom, unable—or unwilling—at first to grasp its meaning. After a long, unbearable moment she spoke.

"Dad's been having an affair with Claire Breen since Graham and I were five years old? How can that be?"

* * *

Behind the restaurant Dana and Gwen strolled a path in a small floral garden of outdoor tables for warm weather dining. Among the array of autumn blooms, they discussed how the man they both loved so much could have successfully carried on a secret romance for seventeen years. And now, did he remember the card he'd hidden away among his old law books? No, he didn't. Or Dana wouldn't have found it. And what about the gift Claire had given him all those years ago, *foolish though it might have been?* Had he forgotten about the gift too? Had he forgotten what he did with it?

"Mom, you think Dad and Claire are still seeing each other?"

"I'm not sure. I drive him everywhere he goes now."

"But what about when you go somewhere without him? You know, like the hairdresser? Or your women's club meetings?"

Dana gulped in a deep breath and shrugged.

"So what now?" asked Gwen.

"I should just divorce him, shouldn't I?"

"My guess? That's easier said than done. You guys

are…you're…forever. So are you going to talk to Dad about this?"

"Not yet. First, I need to know if he and Claire are still together."

* * *

Breakfast the next morning was Dana's favorite blueberry pancakes with crisp bacon and an assortment of fresh fruit. Les had cooked, so she hustled through the cleanup while he swept leaves and other debris off the terrace with the leaf blower going at a low roar. He wore the same old sweats he'd had on the day before. She had on a cashmere sweater and jeans, and sipped coffee from a U of L mug. She watched him for a minute through the window over the kitchen sink. Was this really the man she'd married? The same man who'd been having an affair with his coworker for most of their supposedly wonderful life? Well, perhaps not. Perhaps the guy she'd exchanged vows with was actually another being altogether. Someone from an alien species who came down from outer space to inhabit Les's body and mind. Someone to trick the rest of them into believing that he was a genuine man. As bizarre as that sounded, Dana decided she probably could handle that better than she could cope with his infidelity.

At the built-in computer desk in the breakfast room, the red light blinked on the answering machine. Next to it sat Dana's purse and tote bag. She walked up with an insulated coffee mug and placed it inside the bag. She stepped over to the walk-in pantry and came out with a bag of pretzels and a box of fiber bars—two left—and dropped them inside. She pressed the play button on the machine and listened to the message as she sorted through a stack of magazines on the desk, arranging them in published-date order.

"Hi, sweetie," said her best friend Joan. "Have you checked your e-mails lately? It's that time again. You're heading up our Women's Club Christmas project at the shelter again this year, right? WHW is the best thing we've ever done. Women Helping Women. Love it! You're a genius, sweetie. Talk to you later. Oh, and tell Les now that he's a formal member of the retiree set, Marty's always ready for a weekend golf game. You know my husband. He never lets anything interfere with golf. Call me soon."

Dana added some magazines to the tote bag as the roar of the leaf blower on the terrace wound down and stopped. She hurried out with the bag to put it in her SUV. She was back in the kitchen wiping off the center island with a damp cloth when Les came in from the garage hallway and embraced her from behind. She stiffened, but if he noticed he didn't show it.

"Let's dance," he said. "Remember the first time I said that to you? In the coffee shop around the corner from campus. And we went out and danced up and down the sidewalk in the snow. February, 1980. You remember?"

She eased out of his arms, walked over and left the dish cloth in the sink.

"I don't have time for that right now, Les. But I'm glad your long-term memory is still intact."

She went to the desk, grabbed her purse and swung around. She faced him as if it was the hardest thing she'd ever done. And maybe it was. She'd never lied to him before. But she had to do it now. Because she had to know if he and Claire...

"Off to my bridge club. So...what are your plans for the rest of the day?

Les crossed into the hearth room. "Look what I found in our DVD collection."

He picked up a DVD from the coffee table and came back, showing her the old movie courtroom drama titled "The Verdict" starring the late Paul Newman.

"Don't worry about me," he said. "I've got Newman's film to keep me company. Plus my crossword books. Have fun at bridge, sweetheart. About what time will you be back?"

Dana froze. "Why?"

Les looked puzzled. "Why?"

"Why does it matter what time I'll be back?"

He seemed uncertain. "I…I don't understand."

Dana gave up. She couldn't explain. "I'm not sure what time I'll get back. Before dinner." She started out, and then paused suddenly as she remembered something he'd told her. "You've always said that the Hollywood versions of courtroom drama have so many inaccuracies. Why do you want to watch 'The Verdict' again?"

"It's Newman. You can't beat him. And it's entertainment. Hollywood *can* do that. Sometimes."

Dana nodded and headed out again.

"You forgot to…to kiss me…me good-bye." She paused and he said, "Have you noticed? I'm starting to have trouble saying my words."

Her heart wrenched. He needed her support so much. But she couldn't let that interfere with her quest. She *had* to find out if he and Claire were still seeing each other. So she forced herself to keep going even though her first instinct was to go to him. To comfort him. He was sick and needed her understanding and sympathy. But she couldn't give him what she didn't have right now. Well, she still had those abilities, she just couldn't give them to her husband right now.

"I'm late for bridge, Les."

She hurried off and he gazed after her, bewildered.

"You always kiss me…me…good-bye, sweetheart."

* * *

Dana was backing her SUV out of the garage, when the front door opened and Les came running out past the jack o'lanterns to where she'd stopped in the driveway. She sighed, annoyed, and rolled down the window.

Les said, "I can't find my reading glasses. You know where they are?"

Dana slid the gearshift into park and got out, slamming the door.

Ten minutes later, after finally finding his glasses down between the cushions of his recliner, she backed her SUV into the street and drove off. At the corner she checked for traffic—there wasn't any—and made a U-turn and came back. She parked across the street and down the block a short distance from their house. Beneath the shelter of a drooping tree, leaves floated down on the windshield. She got comfortable behind the wheel and settled in to watch their community come to life. Nobody stirred until after the mail carrier made the rounds, and then one by one the neighbors visited their mailboxes. More time passed and Dana looked at her watch. Eleven-fifteen. She reached into her tote bag on the passenger's seat and brought out her coffee mug. She uncapped it and sipped, gazing out at her house. What was Les doing in there? Did he watch the Paul Newman movie? Had he worked his crossword puzzles? Maybe he'd called Claire and they'd arranged their next rendezvous. And just how would they pull that off now that he wasn't driving anymore?

Dana took a fiber bar from her bag, peeled off the wrapper and munched. A department store delivery truck drove by. Then an elderly couple wearing jackets and hats peddled along on a bicycle built for two. Time dragged. On a lawn down the street, a pair of squirrels played tag in the falling leaves. She put on her glasses and selected a magazine from the tote bag. Her cell phone chirped inside her purse. She took it out and looked at the caller ID before she answered.

"Hi, Gwen."

"So, how are you, Mom?"

"Oh…Angry. Bitter. Resentful. Bored."

Gwen thought about all of that for a minute. "I get everything but the bored part."

"I'm parked down the street from the house spying on your dad. He thinks I'm at my bridge game. I'm trying to catch him with Claire."

"I can't believe that Dad would call her while you're gone and she'd come over to the house. They wouldn't do that. Would they?"

"Three days ago I wouldn't have believed that your dad and Claire were having an affair either. So what I think now is this: he might call her to come and get him and they might…they might go to her place."

Dana choked up. She fought it and kept herself together. She'd had enough of this crying nonsense. How unlike her.

"So how do police detectives do this sort of thing?" she said in a minute. "And private investigators? People who do…surveillance? Isn't that what it's called? How do they handle all the boredom?"

"Mom, I don't know, but I've been thinking. Seventeen years and no one knew about Dad and Claire. *No way*. Somebody saw something. Sometime. Somewhere. That's almost a guarantee. So why hasn't someone let something slip? Or why hasn't anyone felt it was their duty or whatever to inform you?"

"That's not something even your best friend wants to tell

you, honey. And you know what? I'm...Oh...I'm ...I'm..."

When she didn't go on, her daughter said, "Mom? What? You're what?"

"I'm spying on my husband," Dana finally said. "I'm lying to him too."

"And *why* are you doing that?"

"Because he's a cheater!"

CHAPTER 4

At the Connelly's house the dining room was on the right of the foyer in front of the kitchen and butler's pantry. The formal living room was straight ahead beyond the staircase. Les's study occupied the left side of the entrance. The next morning Dana was in there, down on the floor in stretch pants and a sweater going through the two boxes they'd brought home from his law office. The same boxes that she'd suggested he tackle as a way to pass some of the time he had too much of now that he was retired. But he had other ideas about how to spend his leisure hours during the lovely fall weather they'd been having so far. Today was another one of those sunny, cloud-free days with a pleasant breeze sweeping through the trees and the local birds twittering away, apparently not the least bit interested in their annual migration down south.

Through the floor-to-ceiling windows across from the desk, Dana kept an eye on Les grooming the shrubs out front with a pair of hand trimmers, snipping and clacking as he went. He had on the same old sweats he'd worn for the past two days, and she'd have to do something about that soon. She hunted around in the boxes in search of the secret present Claire had given her husband seventeen years ago—*foolish though it might have been* – as Claire had written in her accompanying card. Dana was more than curious about this bit of foolishness and equally anxious to find out what it was. *What* could Claire have given to him?

Les looked happy as a clam on a sandy beach as he worked outside. Watching him through the windows, a pang of regret hit Dana unexpectedly. They weren't a married couple living together anymore, not to her. They were just two acquaintances now coexisting under the same roof. Suddenly, she wanted to be outside with him, poking around in her flower beds, sharing the warm sunlight, enjoying their longtime companionship. But she couldn't do it. Not since she'd found Claire's card and learned that she'd been sharing her husband with someone else for most of their marriage. Instead, she dug into one box and then the other, taking out briefs, motions, trial preparations, notebooks of lawful mumbo-jumbo, folders, legal pads, pens, framed family photos, childhood crafts that Gwen and Graham had made for their dad to proudly display in his office. She finished and repacked the boxes, and then went to work on the desk drawers, finding mostly financial statements, tax forms and old case files. At the bookshelves along the wall, between glances at Les outside, she scrabbled in and among his law books and came up with absolutely nothing.

* * *

A few days later, Les lounged in the hearth room in his recliner. He wore clean sweats and, with his reading glasses perched on his nose, read *The Courier Journal.* Dana, dressed to go out, cleared dishes from the breakfast table in front of the bay window. Per an agreement they had made weeks ago, he did most of the cooking and she handled the clean-up. On the way to the dishwasher, she passed the computer desk and noticed the digital message light blinking on the answering machine. After loading the dishwasher, she came back and pressed the play button, listening to Joan's voice on the recording and sighing, guiltily.

"Hi, sweetie. It's me again. Did you get my other message? Maybe I missed your return call. I sent you another e-mail yesterday. Where are you? I don't want to be a pest, but we need to get cracking on the Christmas project for the shelter. Call me back today, if you can. Bye."

Dana sighed again as Les dropped the newspaper beside his chair. He stood up and stretched before tossing his glasses on the coffee table and heading out. She deleted Joan's message, but not without feeling even guiltier about it. She wasn't up to doing the Christmas project. She wasn't ready to talk to Joan either. Her world had fallen apart and not even her oldest and dearest friend could help her put it back together.

Les returned with the morning mail delivery, grabbed his glasses from the coffee table, and sorted through the stack in the breakfast room. Dana started the dishwasher and he walked over to her holding up a small envelope, the size used for party invitations. He waved it as his wife, but she only gave the envelope a glance. He turned away and left it on the desk for her. She watched him and spoke to his back.

"I'm going shopping this morning."

"I'll go with you, sweetheart."

"No!" Dana yelled. She lowered her voice when he swung around and stared at her. "I'm…getting my nails done too, and some other…oh, you know…girl stuff. What are your plans for today?"

"I don't know. We've still got this great fall weather. I'll find something to keep me busy outside."

Les opened a piece of mail and Dana crossed the room to the back stairs. A picnic in the park with Claire would keep him busy, she wanted to say but didn't.

"Dana, sweetheart, you…you forgot to kiss me good-bye."

She said, "I'm just going up to get my jacket and purse."

She came back downstairs ready to leave. In the hearth room, Les relaxed in his recliner with a crossword puzzle book. He heard her open the garage door.

"Aren't you going to kiss me good-bye?" he called to her.

She ignored him and stepped into the garage and closed the door.

"And I thought I was the one with the…with the …the memory loss," Les said to the empty house.

* * *

Dana's SUV was covered in falling leaves. She'd been sitting at the curb under a spreading tree for hours observing her house. She drank coffee from a thermal mug and flipped pages in a gardening magazine. Her cell phone jingled inside her purse. She took it out and noted the caller ID with a sigh of resignation before she answered.

"Hi, Aunt Nettie."

Nettie McAllister was seventy-five years old and as big around as she was short, which was maybe five feet with her wedges on. She'd covered her bulk in a floral muu-muu and further weighted herself down in gaudy jewelry: around her thick neck, wreathing her ample bosom, circling her big wrists, dangling from her long ears. A profusion of twinkling rubies and emeralds and diamonds. She looked as if she were a tiny, rotund Christmas tree. There was make-up by the pound on her chubby cheeks. Dana's widowed aunt had more money than

Bill Gates. Well, did anybody have more money than Mr. Microsoft? But Aunt Nettie certainly resided in his majestic neighborhood. She and her late husband had made their bounty from small inheritances wisely invested. Primarily in multinational corporations. Aunt Nettie relaxed on a lounger in the sunroom stretched across one side of her mansion in Beaumont Reserve, another affluent Louisville suburb not far from Grand Oaks Village. She cuddled Booboo, her little Yoranian—a cross between a Pom and a York terrier—and rubbed his fury back with tender strokes.

"You're all I've got you know, Dana, my dear," Aunt Nettie said. "The rest of the family doesn't care. They're just waiting for me to die so they can inherit my fortune."

Dana almost groaned. "That's not true, Aunt Nettie."

"Don't give me any of that, my dear. I know better. Well, except for your sweet mother. Are she and your dad still off touring the continent with their inferiors?"

The wealthy old dowager referred to the continent of Europe and to the group of dear friends, none of them as rich as Nettie, with whom Dana's parents often took trips.

"Yes, Aunt Nettie, they're still gone."

"Now, whatever you're doing, I insist you leave it and talk to me." She paused for a breath. "What *are* you doing?"

Dana watched a public school bus roll down the street, stop and discharge two middle-school children. They split up, waving as they separated, and the bus trundled away. Every family in her neighborhood didn't send their children to private school. Some of them believed that the kiddos had to get a dose of reality from somewhere.

"Pay attention to me!" barked Aunt Nettie.

"I always pay attention to you. Even though you don't have a lot to say."

Aunt Nettie boomed with laughter. In a minute she said, "I called to talk about Christmas, my dear."

"Christmas! It's not even Halloween yet! Please, Aunt Nettie, I love you, but I can't talk about the holidays right now."

"Why ever not?"

Dana watched a neighbor leave her house and stroll down the sidewalk to the house next door. She rang the bell. "Because someone's at the door."

"Let the maid answer the door."

"Tilly's not here today. She comes on Mondays and Thursdays. I have to go now, Aunt Nettie. I love you. Bye."

Time almost dragged to a stop after Dana's conversation with her aunt. She chewed on a fiber bar and observed two offspring of the local rabbit family peek out from under the lowest branches of a nearby pine tree. She smiled at the cute babies. As the sun slanted overhead, she yawned and checked her watch. Five-forty. She finished a bag of pretzels and drank the last of her coffee. She gathered the trash into her tote bag and picked up her cell from the console. She punched in a number and waited.

"Hi, Graham. Just wanted to say hello and chat a minute. I'll try you again later, honey. Love you. Bye."

Dana ended the call, but before she could lay down the phone it vibrated in her hand. She'd set it to vibrate when she came out here to snoop. She read the caller ID and answered immediately.

"I thought you'd be studying about now."

Gwen said, "I can't seem to focus today."

"This mess with your dad and me is interfering with school, isn't it? I wish I hadn't said anything to you."

"It's a little late for that. So talk to me. Have you found the mysterious anniversary gift that Claire gave to Dad?"

"Not in what he brought home from the office."

"You think it's at the house somewhere?"

"Wherever he put it, I think he's forgotten all about the gift. I mean just the natural forgetfulness we all begin having as we age, not his dementia."

"You know, Mom, here's a thought: maybe he didn't keep it."

"Good point. Which means I'm just wasting my time looking for it."

* * *

Dana drove her SUV into the garage, hit the remote device hooked over the sunvisor and the big door started rumbling down. Carrying her purse and tote bag, she entered the house and headed for the foyer. All of a sudden, she stopped and went back, remembering that Les thought she'd been out shopping all afternoon. She left the bag under the desk in the breakfast room. He didn't need to see any evidence of how she'd actually spent the day spying on him. She paused by the staircase and watched him at the desk in his study working on the computer. In a minute he glanced up and took off his glasses. He examined her for a time.

"You're back. No shopping bags. That's a first." He smiled. "Couldn't find anything you liked?"

She didn't reply. Just stared at him. What had he been doing all day? Talking on the phone to Claire? Trying to figure out a way to see her without his wife knowing?

"You know, you're e-mails are really piling up. Joan's frantic about something."

Dana nodded and started up the stairs with her purse as the phone rang. Les answered in the study and smiled again, going into a spiel about how good it was to hear from one of his law firm partners. Dana paused on the steps as he went on about surviving retirement, but having a difficult time adjusting to not being a partner anymore. He glanced at his wife and pointed to the phone. He mouthed "Richard" and she climbed another step. Suddenly she stopped. Wait a minute. Was he really talking to Rich? Maybe he hadn't talked to Claire earlier. Maybe she was on the phone now and he didn't want his wife to know. Well, she'd see about that. She left the stairs, hurrying into his office and over to the desk.

"Oh, let me say hi."

She jerked the phone out of Les's hand before he could react. "Hi, Rich. How are you? I'm so glad you called…Rich? Rich?"

She thrust the phone at Les. He fumbled, surprised, and caught it. "Rich, huh?" she said. "So that was Rich. Guess he hung up."

Dana swung around and stalked out. She got as far as the staircase when the phone jingled again. She waited while Les answered. He looked over at her and nodded.

She stared at him. That *had* been Richard? Feeling foolish, she walked back to the desk and accepted the phone from Les.

"Hi, Rich."

"Dana, I'm sorry I cut you off. The cat jumped on my lap and I dropped the phone. Molly likes to surprise me."

* * *

Upstairs in the master suite that evening, Dana rummaged in Les's walk-in closet, foraging for something—anything—that looked as though it didn't belong. Something that Claire gave him, as she had said in her anniversary card—*foolish though it might have been, she hoped this little gift would keep them close to his heart when they weren't together.* Dana checked through Les's hanging clothes and the shelf above.

She opened and closed drawers, tinkering in the contents and finding only bits and pieces of junk: buttons, tie tacks, cuff links, a paper clip. She spun around when footsteps sounded behind her. She faced Les looking as guilty as a thief caught in the act. He examined her, the keen judge of character and behavior that was his forte. Still.

"Cleaning out my closet?" he said. "Why do you look so guilty? It probably needs a good going over." He drew her into his arms. "May I take my lovely wife out to dinner tonight?"

She backed out of his embrace. She didn't want him touching her. The same arms that held Claire. Were they still holding her? Dana didn't even want to be near Les right now. But he didn't seem to notice her attitude. After all, he didn't realize that she now knew about his affair with Claire. He stepped up to his wardrobe and looked it over.

"Let's go somewhere…somewhere…I can't…I don't know…I can't think of the word I want. What is it? Let's go some—"

Dana cut him off. "I don't want to go out tonight."

He glanced at her. "You don't? Why not?"

"Do I have to have a reason?"

Les turned to her, puzzled. "I think so. When someone doesn't want to do something, they usually have a reason."

No comment from his wife. She just glared at him. But he didn't get it.

"You love to go out," he went on. "Are you feeling okay? Maybe you're just in closet-cleaning mode."

She stepped around him and didn't answer. He caught her before she could leave and pulled her back into his arms.

"Dana? Sweetheart?"

She jerked away. She didn't even want to look at him anymore.

"Casual!" he burst out. "That's the word I was trying to think of. Let's just go somewhere casual for dinner. And then after we eat, I thought we could go to that new movie. I don't remember the name of it, but that actor you like stars in it. I remember that. What's his name? Your favorite actor?"

She ignored him and walked out of the closet. He took her silence as agreement and went back to his clothes. He called out to her.

"What should I wear with…with khakis?

No reply from Dana.

"Sweetheart, what should I wear?"

More silence.

"Dana? Sweetheart?'

She charged back into the closet. "Okay! Okay! We'll go!"

"What should I— "

"What about that sweater that Graham and Leah gave you for your birthday?"

"Which sweater did they give me?"

"First, you need to shower before we go. We both do."

"I don't need a shower."

"You only shaved when you got up this morning."

" A shower's not necessary every day."

"Yes, it is. Anyway, we're going out."

"No shower."

She dug in. Deep. This was his daily hygiene, after all. She had to win this battle. And she would. "Okay. If you won't keep yourself clean, I'll just have to call the Home Healthcare folks and ask them to send over an aide to bathe you."

"They do that?"

"Yep. And our insurance will pay for it."

Les stared hard at her. "You'd really call them?"

"Try me."

* * *

The Neighborhood Grill was located in Grand Oaks Village right off the parkway on Appaloosa Way. The parking lot out front wasn't overcrowded, so Dana grabbed a spot near the entrance. Inside, the dining room décor was equine related with pictures of the mottled, western riding horse covering the walls. Appaloosas everywhere. Booths lined the walls, and tables and chairs circled the salad, soup and fruit bar. They sat among the diners at a corner table studying menus while the server returned with their drink orders. A glass of white wine for her, a sudsy mug of beer for him. When the server left with their food order, Les got up and glanced around uncertainly.

"Be right back," he said. "You remember where the restrooms are?"

She nodded toward the restroom sign on the wall across from them and stood.

She reached for her purse. "I'll go with you."

"We can't both go at the same time. Someone might take our table. I'll wait until you come back."

Dana watched him for an instant. It was bad enough that his memory was going, but was he already losing his cognitive skills too?

"Les, nobody will take our table. The hostess seated us. Our drinks are here. Our place settings. Our jackets. This table clearly says occupied. Anyway, the hos—"

He nodded and she stopped, satisfied. He followed her across the dining room as if he were an obedient puppy. Was this too good to be true?

Later, Les worked on a burger and a side salad while Dana picked at her shrimp pasta. Her heart wasn't really in this evening out with her husband, the man who'd betrayed their wedding vows. But finally, she took an interest in how Les kept glancing down at the floor around his chair and under the table. She asked him what was wrong. Well, he couldn't find his napkin, he explained. It was only paper and somehow it just kept flitting away. When their server stopped by with drink refills, Les wound up with a small stack of napkins, which he proceeded to go through as though there was no tomorrow. His hamburger was medium rare and quite juicy. Delicious. Messy. But his disappearing napkins were a nuisance. The soiled ones piled up around his plate. The clean ones were nowhere to be found.

"I can't find my napkin," he said.

"Imagine that," she replied. "Did you check your lap?"

He checked. Nothing on his khakis down there. He finished his salad, and then said, "Dana, sweetheart, don't I have a napkin?"

She gulped a ragged sigh, but what she really wanted to do was cut loose with one of those Tarzan yells. Even a hyena scream would help. Her patience with Les and his dementia was fading faster than a sunset over the Gulf of Mexico. Instead of yelling and screaming, she took a tissue from her purse and offered it to him.

"Thanks."

In a minute Les said, "Edward Norton."

Dana stared at him.

"Your favorite actor. I've been trying to think of his name."

He reached into his lap for the expected napkin—he had no memory of the tissue—and came up with the tissue.

"Don't I have a napkin?"

"In your lap."

"So what's this?" He held the tissue out to her.

Dana ground her teeth and clenched her jaw, but she didn't say anything until she got a grip on her emotions.

"Les, you're taking your meds every morning, right?"

He nodded, dropping the tissue among the soiled napkins. "Why?"

"I just asked."

"I'm not doing very well, am I?"

"Not tonight."

She would have to start paying attention to his prescription bottle. She should have been doing that all along. She hadn't yet become accustomed to her dementia-victim husband with his failing memory and waning common sense. She'd grown much too content with her intelligent, responsible, perceptive, considerate and loving spouse. Well, Les was still considerate and loving. But selfishly, perhaps, she wanted the whole man back again. Although, she didn't want Claire along with him.

Their server arrived with hot coffee and a dessert cart. She cleared the table mess while Les selected a large slice of chocolate cake. Dana moaned and searched among the choices and located a low-calorie dish of fresh fruit. The server retreated and they started in with relish. A few minutes later Les finished his dessert and fumbled about, looking everywhere, on the table, in his lap.

"I've lost my napkin." He glanced down at the floor. "Oh, there it is. I dropped it. You think I can get another one?"

She glowered across the table at him, but what she really wanted to do was lean across and slap him silly. She really needed to work on her patience.

He read her sullen expression, but didn't understand and said, "What?"

She didn't respond and he just watched her for a time, bewildered. Then a mixture of emotions played over his face. Anger. Sadness. Frustration. Even a flash of hope lit in there somewhere.

"I'm in real trouble, aren't I?" he asked. "I mean, it's no longer just memory loss, is it? My cognitive skills are going too."

He looked away, out across the dining room. At the accommodating hostess, the attentive servers. At the departing diners and the new arrivals.

At last his eyes came back to her. "I wonder when they'll bring the dessert cart."

CHAPTER 5

A week later Dana stood in her dressing room off the master suite, putting on a pair of khakis and a sweater. As she stepped into her loafers, Les appeared in the doorway in his boxers and T-shirt.

"Where did you say we're going, sweetheart?" he asked.

"You have an appointment with the neurologist this morning."

"What for?"

She explained that the appointment was a routine check-up on how his dementia was progressing. The doctor would perform some tests, and then he and Les would talk about the results. A doctor visit was out of Les's daily comfort zone, and he became upset all of a sudden. Dana assured him that she would be there too, although only for the discussion afterwards, not the tests.

"Why can't you stay with me during the tests?"

"Probably because I'd be a distraction. This is something you have to do totally on your own."

"Why?"

"Because you're the patient."

He nodded and strolled out. Abruptly, he came back.

"What should I wear?"

"Casual."

A few minutes later, she arranged her hair and checked her make-up at the mirror over the vanity. She caught his reflection when he strode up behind her. He had on one of the business suits he used to wear at his law office.

She said, "What's with the suit? What happened to casual?"

"I know I have an appointment today. I just can't remember where, so I…I thought…I guess I thought—" He stopped, frustrated. "I don't know what I thought."

Dana reminded Les that he had an appointment with his neurologist and suggested that he follow her lead when it came to what he'd wear. He considered her khakis and sweater carefully before walking into the bedroom.

Later, at the computer desk in the breakfast room, he wore his glasses and sorted through the morning mail. He had on Dockers and a cable-knit sweater. She joined him, taking her car keys out of her purse. She wore a jacket and carried his jacket over her arm. He glanced up and asked where she was going. She released a long, deep sigh. Patience, she reminded herself. She had to have patience with him.

"*We* are going to your neurologist appointment."

"Okay. As soon as I finish with the mail."

She consulted her watch. "Look at the time. We need to go, Les."

He ignored her. "You've got an old piece of mail lying here. Looks like a party invitation from your friend, Geneva."

"We'll be late for your appointment with Dr. Heyburn. You can finish the mail when we get back."

"Why can't I finish it now?"

"I just told you," she replied. "We don't have time. Let's keep our priorities straight here. The mail can wait a couple of hours."

Les slapped down an envelope. "Are you saying I…I've got my…my priorities messed up?"

He jerked off his reading glasses and dropped them on the desk. He jumped up and slammed around her and out into the hallway leading to the garage. She closed her eyes and pulled in a slow, seething breath. She had to remember that dementia not only caused memory loss, it caused errors in judgment too.

* * *

Returning later from the neurologist's office in nearby Lakewood, Dana drove her SUV off I-71 East at the Grand Oaks exit. Her headlights cut through the gray early afternoon and steadily falling rain. The perfect harbinger of how she felt after the lengthy wait to see Dr. Heyburn, but at least his examination had resulted in good news.

Dana's cell phone chirped down in her purse, and Les asked if she wanted him to answer the call. She nodded and he picked up her purse lying on the console, fumbling through the contents. He removed Claire's anniversary card in its envelope and laid it on the console, flap side up. Dana glanced over and saw the envelope. She tensed and stared at her husband for a minute. He poked around, found her cell and studied the caller ID, unconcerned with the envelope. He let out a weary sigh. He didn't remember how to use her phone. He didn't even know where he had put his own cell phone.

"How do I answer this thing? It's your Aunt Nettie."

Dana showed him which button to push, and he placed the phone to his ear.

"Hi, Aunt Nettie. How are you?" He gazed out the side window at the steady rain. "I'm sorry you're not well. I hope you feel better soon. Dana's right here, but I'm afraid she can't talk right now. I don't think she likes to drive and use the phone at the same time. Not the safest thing to do, you know."

Les reached idly for the envelope as he listened to Aunt Nettie's chatter. Dana noticed and her tension level ramped up. He dropped it and she drew a grateful breath.

"Dana will call you back when we get home...Aunt Nettie? Hello? Hello?" He looked over at his wife. "She hung up on me." He shook his head. "What a character."

Laughing, Les dropped the phone back in Dana's purse. He picked up the envelope again. The flap side was still up. She glanced at him and stopped breathing.

"What's this, sweetheart?" he asked, about to turn the envelope over.

Nonchalantly, she eased her hand over for it and tucked the thing back inside her purse. She fabricated that one of the reasons Joan kept calling her and sending e-mails was because she'd run out of stamps. And she'd asked Dana to mail the card since she was on her way to the post office anyway.

"Joan thinks I forgot to mail it."

"She's right," Les said.

"Oh...well...yes...I mean...no...that is...I'm *going* to mail it."

Les stared out the windshield, watching the downpour. She held her breath. Would he move on to something else now?

"Sweetheart, I...I know we've just come from seeing the neurologist, right? But tell me again what he said."

Yes!

"Dr. Heyburn said that your dementia is typical of most of his cases. You have good days as well as days that aren't as good. And, overall, the disease is progressing slowly. That's good news, don't you think?"

"I'm so glad to be doing as well as I am, but good news

would be that I'm cured. That would be great news. But there's no cure, is there?"

"Not yet."

"How's the research going?"

"About like your disease. Slow."

* * *

The next morning Dana sat in her SUV across the street and down the block from their house. She was back on surveillance duty sheltered beneath a tree, but facing in the opposite direction now. She'd changed locations hoping that her constant presence at the curb wouldn't rouse a neighbor's curiosity. The weather still wasn't that cold for fall and sun splashed through the shuffling clouds. Wearing comfortable sweats, she stayed toasty warm. She sipped from her coffee mug and took in the action in their little corner of the world. But there wasn't much going on so far today.

A jogger passed. And then an Eldorado pick-up chugged by with a big, blond lab snuffling the brisk breeze from the truck bed. Time crawled and Dana yawned and glanced at her watch. A UPS delivery van came along and wheeled into the next door neighbor's driveway and parked. A uniformed man hopped out carrying a large package. He tapped the doorbell and left the parcel on the porch. A little girl on a shiny pink and purple scooter whizzed past keeping warm inside a fuzzy sweater and ear muffs. Another neighbor's door opened and the man of the house reached out and checked the mailbox for the day's quota. He carried it inside with both hands.

Dana reached into her tote bag for a magazine when a white Mercedes drove up and swung into their driveway and stopped. Dana gasped as a petite woman got out with her purse. Joan Reidling had on jeans and a matching jacket. She was in her fifties and as trim as a dieting teenager, with beautiful dark eyes and not a silvery hair out of place. Joan had intelligence and energy to spare, and she used much of it to work tirelessly for the Grand Oaks Women's Club and its many worthwhile projects.

Dana jammed her coffee mug into the console drink holder and leaped out of her SUV as if it had suddenly caught fire. She raced down the sidewalk and up to the house, intercepting her best friend before she could ring the bell. Joan paused in surprise on the steps and turned.

"Oh, I keep forgetting to call you, Joanie!" Dana glibly lied. "I'm so sorry!"

Joan gave Dana's sweats and athletic shoes the once over. "You've been running? You're in great shape, sweetie. You're not even breathing hard."

Dana nodded and stared at her oldest friend. How she hated all this lying. She glanced at the door. She had to get Joan away from here before Les heard them.

She said, "I need to wind down. Walk with me."

Joan left her purse in her car and joined Dana. They strolled down the block in the opposite direction of Dana's SUV.

"You're having a difficult time with Les and his dementia, aren't you?" asked Joan, her voice filled with sympathy.

"Sometimes it's harder than other times, yes."

"You're a caregiver now, not just a wife. Although, have you ever noticed how closely related those two positions are?"

Dana and Joan looked at each other and smiled.

"I can't even imagine all of your stress," Joan continued. "So is Les's situation getting worse?"

"Oh...you could say that."

When Joan asked Dana if the women's club Christmas

project at the shelter would be too much for her this year, her friend sighed with relief. They paused on their walk and hugged, and then Dana apologized for what she couldn't do, but Joan would have none of that. She would find a replacement. A challenge but doable.

They walked on and Joan said, "Did you get the shower invitation?"

"I think so. Geneva's son's getting married, isn't he? I'll check the registry and have a gift delivered."

When they arrived back at Dana's house, they stopped in the driveway beside Joan's Mercedes. She examined her dear friend carefully.

"Are you sure you're okay?"

Dana lied again with a quick nod and a phony smile. Joan didn't buy it.

"Have you considered joining one of those help groups for caregivers? I've been told they're actually a big help."

"Not really. I...oh, I don't know, Joanie..."

When Dana didn't go on, Joan said, "You're not telling me all of it, are you? Okay. But call me if you need anything. Help with Les. Anything at all. That's one of the privileges of being president of the women's club. I get to delegate and free up more of my own time. So call me, even if it's just to unload a bit. You know you can tell me anything, and I'm always just brimming with advice."

Dana faked another smile and hugged Joan before she left. She watched her friend climb in her car, start up and back down the driveway. They waved at each other, and then Joan was gone. Dana sighed with gratitude. She got all the way back to her SUV before it hit her how wrong that felt.

* * *

The following day started out cloudy and chilly, but with the promise of pure sunlight and warm temperatures before nightfall. Dana wore a clean pair of sweats and sat at the curb in her SUV flipping magazine pages when a Speedy Ride taxicab eased past and turned into their driveway. She glanced up and hunched down in her seat. She tossed the magazine aside. What was this? Why had Les called a cab? Where was he going? To meet Claire?

Only one way to find out. Peeking over the steering wheel, she watched him come out of the house still dressed in the old sweats he'd put on that morning. He'd added a beat up corduroy jacket and a tattered fishing hat. He looked ridiculous. Did he think he was in disguise?

The cab driver jumped out to open the rear door for Les. He slid into the back seat, and the driver closed the door. He got behind the wheel again and backed into the street. Dana hunched down in the seat again as the taxi whipped off. Then she was up and turning the key in the ignition. She zipped along after them.

She trailed the taxicab along I-71 West into downtown Louisville. She followed it onto River Road and wound up behind the cab in the parking lot at River Road Landing, the marina where their son lived and worked. She parked among the other vehicles out by the road and watched the cab draw up to the wharf. Graham stood there waiting in worn jeans and a hoodie with the marina logo on the front. Les climbed out of the back seat, and the driver rolled down his window. Les paid the man and he zoomed off, presumably to pick up his next fare. Les and Graham hugged. Dana opened her window so she could eavesdrop on their conversation as it drifted over on the cool breeze.

Graham said, "Sorry I couldn't come and get you, Dad, but

Dallas borrowed my car. He's got a job interview."

"Why aren't you working today, son? You're employed, right?"

"I help out around here when they need me, but I'm off today. So we can get in some good fishing."

"We're going fishing?"

Graham slid an arm around his father's shoulders and they started along the wharf toward a large houseboat. He waved at a couple shoving off in their cabin cruiser.

"That's the plan, Dad."

"I didn't bring any gear."

"I've got everything already loaded on the boat."

Dana watched them board a houseboat decorated with anchors, life preservers and fishnet, listening as the motor started up. She watched Graham expertly back the boat from its slip into the river, and then head upstream before digging in her purse for her cell phone. She selected a number and waited.

"Hi, Gwen. Guess where your dad is."

* * *

Dana sat at the computer desk in the breakfast room the following morning catching up on her e-mails. Les walked up.

"You want to go for a run, sweetheart?" he asked.

"I want to finish these e-mails."

"I'll wait for you."

"You go ahead," she said. "I'm going to be a while."

When he just stood there, she looked up over the top of her glasses and noticed that he had on the same sweats he'd worn for the past two days. He smelled like fish from his adventure with Graham yesterday. And it *had* been an adventure for him. He chattered nonstop about all the fish they'd caught and tossed back. She was glad that he'd had so much fun and that he remembered it, but she was heartily sick of the smell and decided to get rid of it.

"Why didn't you put on clean clothes after your shower?"

Les stared at her, thinking that over. "Did I take a shower this morning?"

"Yes…well…after our battle."

She explained—again—that personal hygiene had become a problem for him. Just one more problem dementia victims and their families had to struggle with, but the doctors didn't seem to know why this one was such a serious issue.

"Why don't you toss those sweats down the laundry shoot for Tilly to wash and put on a clean pair?"

He examined his sweats. "What's wrong with these?"

"Well…they're dirty. You wore them fishing. They smell."

"Fishing? I went fishing? Who…who…with Graham?"

"Les, will you please just go up and change?"

"I don't want to change," he replied, sounding like a whiney two-year-old, which suddenly gave her an idea.

"Please, Les. I'll give you a special treat if you do."

His demeanor changed so quickly that she barely had time to process it. Ah-oh.

With a healthy gleam of sexual lust in his eyes, he said, "What kind of special treat do you have in mind?"

Well, so much for the sniveling two-year-old. She now had a rutting stag on her hands. And making his favorite breakfast, the treat she'd vaguely had in mind, just wouldn't cut it. She was about to start worrying, then suddenly realized something: Les had been going out for a run and by the time he got back—probably *before* he got back—this conversation would be forgotten. She released a thankful sigh and smiled.

"You may choose any treat you want after you get back."

"Now…now…where am I going?"

"Out for a run."

"Oh, right. Out for my run. You want to go with me?"

"No. I need to finish these e-mails."

"Okay." He bent down and pecked her cheek.

"Don't forget to go up and change first."

He nodded. "Right."

She watched him depart for the back stairs and sighed with relief. She was doing a lot of this sighing business lately.

* * *

Les jogged down the sidewalk in front of the house. At the next cross street, he hung a left. He jogged past two more cross streets and turned at the third intersection. Half way along he paused and looked uncertain, gazing around at a few passing vehicles. He started to panic when he spotted the mail carrier's nifty little white truck with red and blue striped trim slowing at a row of curbside mailboxes. He hurried over to the curb. The woman behind the wheel slid her door open.

"Morning, Les," she said with a smile.

"Morning…uh…Connie!" Les glanced about, looking helpless now. "I think I…I'm…I seem to…uh…Connie, can you tell me how to get back…back to the house?"

The mail carrier nodded with understanding. Grand Oaks Village was a small community, although not so small that everyone knew everyone else. Just close enough that public service folks as well as residents came to know a little bit about a lot of people's business. She'd heard Les's unfortunate story and it saddened her.

"Sure, Les," she said. "Go back two streets and take a right. Then go three streets and take a left. Your place is down on the left. About seven houses."

Les looked as lost as the proverbial ball in tall weeds.

Connie said, "Two streets back. Take a right. Go three more streets and take a left. Seven houses down on the left. That's your place. You'll see it."

The mail carrier waved and drove on. Les went back the way he came, just strolling now and counting. He was focused only on Connie's directions.

"Two streets right. Three streets left. Seven houses down. Two streets right. Three streets left. Seven houses down."

The directions became a chant that built up a rhythm. His entire body going with the flow. He concentrated so hard that he didn't notice anything else and crossed one street directly in the path of an oncoming Lincoln Continental. The driver swerved and missed him. Barely. But the man didn't blow his horn. He recognized Les-the-renowned-defense-attorney, and shook his head, giving him the benefit of the doubt.

The doorbell chimed through the house with a melodic tinkling. Dana ignored it and went on typing an e-mail reply at the computer. When the bell tinkled a second time she called out.

"Tilly, can you get that, please!"

In a minute Dana dropped her glasses on the desk and jumped up. What was she thinking? The maid wasn't here today. In the foyer she checked the viewer and opened the door. Les stood there in a dither. Bewildered. Frustrated. Shaking. He gulped in breath after breath, like a person who'd been denied oxygen for too long.

"I couldn't...I couldn't..." he stammered. "I... I couldn't... I..."

She said, "Les. Stop. Just stop. Take a deep breath."

He did and she told him to take several more. When he had

calmed, she reached for his hand, drawing him inside. She closed the door, let go of his hand, and studied him until his breathing returned to normal.

"Tell me what happened," she said.

"I don't know what happened…I just…I don't know…I can't…"

"I know. You can't remember. But maybe we can piece it together."

Suddenly, Les dug into his pockets, frantic again, searching. Remembering some of it. "I couldn't find my way back." He offered her his empty hands. "I guess I lost my house keys too. How did I do that?"

Dana walked over to the long side table next to the staircase. "No, here they are. Right where you always keep them."

He joined her and took his keys from a decorative dish. He examined them with a frown. "Where's the key to my car?"

"You don't drive anymore. We sold your car."

He dropped the keys back in the dish. He remembered now. Selling his Audi. He couldn't remember where he lived, but he sure hadn't forgotten his white Audi TT Roadster. He'd loved that car. Still did. Always would. He swung around, shoulders sagging, and ambled through the foyer, past his study to the living room at the back of the house. He'd lost his short-term memory and now his independence was gone. How long until he was completely useless?

CHAPTER 6

Early that evening logs flamed in the fireplace in the hearth room. In front of the floor-to-ceiling windows facing the back lawn, a pair of recliners sat on each side of an end table with a tall lamp. Seated in a recliner with the remote, Dana searched channels on the big-screen TV across the room. In the background through the windows light faded from the sky. Wearing his old corduroy jacket over his sweats, Les filled the bird feeders hanging from the spreading tree limbs. He carried a plastic bucket of seed that he dipped out with a handled scoop. On the ground birds followed him from tree to tree, pecking the seeds that dropped and scattered as he moved. Dana settled in with an ocean-life documentary and watched a school of dolphins streaming through the water. When Les finished feeding the birds and came in, she was absorbed in a baby dolphin's birth. He left his seed bucket by the garage door and slung his jacket on a wall peg in the closet. In the half bath, he washed and dried his hands before heading into the kitchen. He helped himself to a glass of water from the door dispenser in the fridge, and then opened the double doors and checked out the dinner choices.

"I made this vegetable soup, didn't I?" he asked. "Shall

we...we have the rest of it for dinner tonight?"

Dana mumbled something unintelligible and Les closed the door, strode over and flopped down in the empty recliner. He stared at the cavorting dolphins on TV.

"After your program goes off, let's drive up to the bakery and get a loaf of that crusty French bread you like so much."

She swung around and stared at him. "You remember that." It wasn't a question.

He met her gaze with a wicked smile. "You might be surprised at what all I remember. Like how much you enjoy spontaneous sex. I could ravage you right here on the couch if you want."

She choked on a phony cough to keep from laughing. If he only knew just how much his idea appealed to her. But she still didn't want to be intimate with her husband.

"Not now, Les."

He settled back in his chair to watch the rest of the documentary with her. She just stared at the TV screen now, not seeing, not hearing, just remembering.

* * *

It was late on a mild June night about twelve years ago. Dana led Les beneath the trees on their back lawn to a camping tent he'd helped the kids set up at the rear of the property. They both had on bathrobes. She pulled back the door flap to the tent, revealing two sleeping bags laid out together in the glow of several pillar candles arranged on pedestals. On a small table sat a slender goblet, a champagne bottle wedged into a bucket of ice, and a bowl of fresh grapes.

"Come into my boudoir said the lady to the gent," she beckoned.

"Are you sure the kids are still at summer camp?"

She giggled like a kid herself as he shut the door flap. He got comfortable on the sleeping bags while she poured the champagne. Plucking one grape from the bunch, she knelt and dipped it into the goblet. She fed her mate, letting her robe fall open and showing him that she had on nothing underneath. His eyes filled with desire. She put the champagne glass back on the table. He slid off her robe, and then his own.

* * *

Les stood in his pajamas on the balcony off the master suite, hugging himself against the chill in the morning air and taking in the rhythms of the invigorating new day. When he'd had enough of the backyard view, he walked back inside. He found Dana in the adjoining bathroom brushing her teeth at the sink in the vanity. She observed as he took his meds from the vial in the cabinet, drew a glass of water and swallowed. He set the glass down and looked at her.

"I've spent most of my adult life in either an office or a courtroom," he said. "I think I'll enjoy getting acquainted with the outdoors again. That part not included on a golf course. So what's on your agenda today, sweetheart?"

Around her toothbrush, she said, "Hair appointment."

"I think I'm playing golf with Pete and Richard."

She stared at him in the mirror for a minute before rinsing her toothbrush. Was he playing golf with his partners? Or was he planning to sneak in some time with his lover while his wife was at the hair salon?

"You remember making plans with Pete and Rich?" she asked, putting her toothbrush away and reaching for the bottle of mouthwash.

"No, but Pete left a reminder message on…on the machine

downstairs after you went to bed last night."

"We went to bed at the same time."

"We did? I think I got back up. Maybe the phone woke me."

"Did you erase the message? Never mind. I know you don't remember. Well, you'd better shave and shower. I wonder what time they're picking you up?"

"I don't need to shave and shower before I play golf."

Dana rinsed her mouth and put away the mouthwash. She left the bathroom without commenting. She was dealing with a dementia victim now, she reminded herself, not just a husband, and she had to pick her battles. And they'd had this one too many times before. Les trailed her into the bedroom and over to her closet.

"Speaking of golf," she said, "Joan told me that Marty's always good for a weekend game. You remember Joan's husband, don't you?"

"I think so. I'll give him a call right now. Maybe he'd like to join us today. Where do you have their phone number?"

"On my cell phone."

"That thing confuses me now. I don't even know what I did with mine."

He sat down on the bed and picked up the house extension as she recited Joan and Marty's home phone number from memory. She knew where his cell phone was, but wouldn't mention it. In the drawer of his bedside table. And she'd checked the phone thoroughly. Not many calls over the years between him and Claire. Of course, some were to be expected. Business-related conversations since they had worked in the same law office. But there wasn't an excess of calls. So they had been cautious regarding personal talks. And why not? They'd had eight plus hours a day, five days a week to say anything they wanted.

* * *

At the computer desk Dana found a phone message from Pete saying that he'd be along in about an hour. Wearing a brown jacket over tan Dockers and a sweater, Les strolled up behind her relating that he'd reached Marty, who was delighted to join them at the country club golf course. She thought about that for a minute. Les, Pete, Richard and Marty. A nice foursome. Or was it? Five could play just as well.

Forty-five minutes later, she was dressed to go out in black stretch pants and a yellow turtleneck. She observed from the front window in Les's study as he walked outside past the grinning jack o'lanterns and climbed into Pete's red Porsche waiting in the driveway. Okay. She hurried out, grabbed her purse from the table in the foyer and headed for the garage.

She trailed Les and Pete along the parkway in her SUV, staying several cars back in traffic so she wouldn't be noticed. She followed them through Grand Oaks Village onto Shady Lake Drive, past the meandering lake to Oakwood Lane. In the country club parking lot, she lurked among the other vehicles and watched Pete park and get out with her husband. They strolled up to the clubhouse and met Richard going in just as Marty joined them from across the lot. Marty was the short one of the group with graying hair and blue eyes. The perfect match for his petite wife Joan.

Dana knew that Claire drove a gray Lexus. She searched the parking area and didn't find one. She slipped into an empty spot and waited. And waited. Checking her watch, she took out her cell phone, selected a number and pushed a button. She waited some more.

"Hi, Wanda, it's Dana. I'm running a little late for my appointment. I'm sorry. Do we need to reschedule? ... Are you sure? ... Okay, if you're sure... I'll see you in about fifteen minutes. How's that?"

She ended the call and made another one.

"Hi, Gwen. Guess where your dad is, honey." She explained, adding, "I thought Claire might be coming to the golf game. But now I don't think so. Men need to have their own time together just as women do."

"I think that's called testosterone without any annoying estrogen," Gwen said. "You know, Mom, you've been spying on Dad for two weeks now. I don't think he's still seeing her. I know that's not much consolation."

"Spying on your dad. Because I can't trust him anymore. Twenty-five years of trust. Gone in the time it took me to read Claire's card."

* * *

In the recreation room on the lower level of the Connelly's house, a pool table occupied one side of a huge open area and a ping pong table stood on the other side. The steps coming down from the kitchen divided the space. Storage cabinets lined the two end walls. That afternoon Dana scoured through the cabinets, searching for something—anything—that didn't look familiar or didn't appear to belong. Something that Claire might have given to Les. Dana came across everything from cheap souvenirs to old cookbooks. She found the family picture album and opened it. In a vacation snapshot taken about fifteen years ago by an obliging neighbor, she and Les with Gwen and Graham stood by their SUV, ready to leave on a road trip. She gazed at the picture and remembered.

* * *

It was a hot, sunny July morning. Les drove I-65 South. Dana rode in the passenger's seat; Gwen and Graham sat in the back. The family sang an old novelty song that mom and dad had taught the kids titled "Would You Like To Swing On A Star."

Dana and Les started it off. "Would you like to swing on a star/carry moonbeams home in a jar/and be better off than you are/or would you rather be a mule?"

Gwen and Graham took over. "A mule is an animal with long, funny ears/kicks up at anything he hears/his back is brawny but his brain is weak/he's just plain stupid with a stubborn streak."

Dana and Les finished up. "And by the way, if you hate to go to school/you may grow up to be a mule."

Beneath a tree in a rest area along the interstate, Dana took food dishes out of a big cooler sitting on a shady picnic table. Les cooked burgers for lunch on a portable grill, and the kids arranged place settings with paper plates, napkins and utensils.

"This is great, isn't it?" Les asked, flipping a burger. "I love my job, but you guys are my life. So how many more miles to the beach, Mom?"

* * *

Dana came back from her memories with a jolt. She closed the album and thought about Les. She opened the photo album again and leafed through to a favorite picture of her husband. She glared at him.

"If we were your life, then why did you need someone else?"

This time she slammed the album shut, wondering if all lawyers were as good at lying as Les was. Didn't it come with the territory? Footsteps on the stairs made her glance up. Les came slowly down balancing a steaming coffee mug that said WORLD WIDE WOMEN—WOW. He came over to her. She placed the family album back in the cabinet and stood up. She relieved him of the mug and they went over to a set of old living room furniture arranged around a bare coffee table and took seats on the sofa. Across from them a small kitchen was built into a wall with French doors going out to the backyard. A table and four chairs sat before the doors.

He said, "I peeked down at you a while ago. You looked lost in the past with that old album, so I decided not to…to bother you."

She blew at her mug and sipped. "Thanks for the coffee."

"Tell me something," he said. "If…if you could go back and do it all over again, would you still marry me?"

She stared at him. She stared *through* him. When the phone clanged, they both looked into the kitchen at the vintage wall phone hooked up there, the kind with a rotary dial, a pair of loud bell ringers, and the receiver attached at the end of a length of cord.

"I'll get it," he said.

She watched him and thought of that old maxim—saved by the bell. He answered and immediately turned to face her.

"Hello, Aunt Nettie," he said.

She shook her head, and then changed her mind and got up. Better to deal with her aging aunt than to answer her husband's question. If he still remembered it. But when she took the phone from him, Aunt Nettie only wanted to talk about Christmas and Dana put her off again with a promise to call back after Halloween.

That night she was reading in bed while Les made getting-ready-for-bed noises in the bathroom: Flushing toilet. Running water. Dropping something on the floor. Have you seen my toothbrush? Now, what did I do with the toothpaste? Dana, sweetheart, can you come in here? She sighed dramatically. She might as well be raising a third child. Even raising twins again would be easier than coping with Les's dementia. She placed her book on the night table with her glasses and got up, thinking that she hadn't really been reading just now as much as turning pages. All she could really focus on, most of the time now, was Les and their twenty-five happy years of family life. And why had he wanted—needed—Claire too. Why? *Why?*

Back in bed Dana was reading when Les snuggled in next to her. She tensed and edged away. He didn't get the message.

"I love the way you smell," he said. "What is it when we go to bed?"

She sighed again and closed the book, ignoring his question. "Les, tell me something. Are you happy with me?"

"I certainly am."

She gave him a sidelong look. Was that the truth? Or one of his lawyer lies?

"What would you change about me?"

"Nothing, sweetheart."

"There must be something. I'm hardly perfect."

"I didn't say you were perfect. I said I wouldn't change you."

He tugged her closer and kissed the side of her neck. "I know I'm failing mentally, but I…I haven't forgotten how to show you how much I love you."

She pushed him away. "No, Les, not tonight."

He lay beside her, troubled. He didn't understand and didn't know what to do about it. He laid there until he soon didn't remember what was bothering him, and then rolled over and went to sleep. Innocent as a child. She finally relaxed next to him, but she didn't go to sleep for a long time.

* * *

Late the next afternoon, Les sat at the desk in his study. Reading glasses on, he stared at the computer screen, trying to reconcile the bank statement for their household account. He frowned as Dana wandered in and she asked him what was wrong. He explained that the bank had made a mistake somewhere in their monthly procedure and he couldn't figure out exactly how somebody had messed up. When she offered to take a look, he exploded at her.

"I can still—" He stopped, suddenly flustered. "I can…I…what's the word I want? I can still…"

"Les, what are you talking about?"

She stepped around behind him and looked at the computer screen.

"Rec…rec…reconcile. That's the word. I can still reconcile our bank account, Dana. You think I've turned into an idiot overnight? I'll figure this out."

"Of course you will."

"For heaven's sake! Don't patronize me!"

Startled at his outburst, she stared at him for an instant before she whipped around and beat a hasty retreat. Boy, was he in a mood! He found her a few minutes later at the kitchen sink, washing fresh lettuce and tearing it into a salad bowl. He embraced her from behind. She stiffened.

"I'm sorry," he said, turning her around to face him. "I yelled at you a while ago, didn't I? Please forgive me, sweetheart. We don't do that, do we?"

She nodded, dripping water on him from the lettuce leaves and pulling away. She couldn't remember him ever raising his voice. Not to her. Not to the children.

He watched her go back to the sink and the salad. "Dana,

what's wrong with us? We're not like we used to be, are we?"

She didn't reply, just shut off the running water.

"Dana, will you answer me, please?"

"I need some time right now, Les," she said without looking at him.

"Time for what?"

"No questions right now. Just give me some time."

* * *

Dana was stretched out in her recliner in the hearth room early the following evening holding an ice pack to her forehead. The windows behind her were ajar and the warm October air felt good as the sun slid gracefully below the distant tree line. She overheard Les on the back lawn. He pruned a rose bush and talked college sports with a neighbor: University of Louisville basketball versus University of Kentucky basketball. Both teams had been national champions in previous years, U K several times and U of L just last year. And who would make the best showing in the upcoming competitions? Either way, the state of Kentucky would be well represented, both men agreed.

The phone jangled as Les came inside through the French doors in the breakfast room. He glanced over at Dana and laid his pruning shears on the table. He took the call at the phone on the computer desk.

"Hello…Pete! How are you, buddy?...Sure. Sounds good…What…No, last minute's okay. Just let me check with Dana." He faced her and noted the ice pack on her head. "I'll call you right back."

He hung up and walked over to his wife. "What's wrong, sweetheart?"

"My headache's worse."

"Did you tell me you had a headache?"

"I think so."

"And I forgot. I'm sorry. Pete and Gloria want us to meet them for dinner at the *Seafood Shack*. I'll tell Pete we can't make it."

She sat up removing the ice pack. "No, I'll go. I feel a little better. Maybe if I get my mind on something else."

"No, sweetheart. I'll tell Pete—"

"I can go, Les."

"No—"

"I said I can go."

"Dana, sweet—"

"I said I can go, Les! Don't be such a jerk! I can go! I can go!"

Suddenly, she burst into tears and he looked dumbfounded. For a minute he didn't know how to react. A sobbing wife wasn't anyone he'd ever had to deal with before. And he didn't think she'd ever called him a jerk either. But a basic instinct to offer comfort kicked in and he wrapped her in his arms while she cried. He wanted to make her feel better with words too, but he couldn't think how to say them. Dana was one of the strongest people he knew, although, right now she seemed to need some of his strength. But he wasn't sure exactly how to give it to her. His thoughts were getting all jumbled up. Maybe if he just held on quietly, she'd soon be okay. Sometimes the greatest strength was just in being there, just offering support. He recalled that from his law practice. His clients wanted—needed—his advice, of course, his knowledge, his training, his courtroom expertise, but sometimes they just needed *him*. How he missed that!

* * *

The University of Louisville campus was beautiful all year round. But especially in the fall when the trees put on their lovely changing routine and decorated the landscape in brilliant shades of orange and gold and red. Halloween afternoon Dana and Gwen strolled along a shady path scattered with falling leaves and hurrying students. There was a bite in the air and Dana had on brown wool pants and an ivory sweater. Gwen wore jeans and a long-sleeve gray hoodie air-brushed with a half-body shot of her favorite sports celebrity, Most Outstanding Player of 2013 NCAA Final Four, Luke Hancock. Luke, in a black uniform, gripped the ball during a game and checked out the possibilities for one of his famous three-point shots.

"I guess Dad remembers his affair with Claire," Gwen said. "I mean if they aren't together anymore, if one or both of them decided to end it, that has to be a recent thing. And they did it because of Dad's memory loss."

"I'm sure he remembers the affair, honey. Dr. Heyburn explained that emotional memory is different from other kinds of memory. That it takes a separate path in the brain. Your dad will recall his relationship with Claire for a lot longer than he'll remember…oh…say…a movie we saw last week. Of course, already he can't remember if we saw a movie *yesterday*."

"Mom, have you decided if you're going to divorce Dad or not?"

"I don't know. If I don't, then I've got to be able to forgive him. I can't just carry all this around, pretending I don't know. As I'm doing now. Your dad is sick and all I want to do is scream at him."

"Why was he with Claire for seventeen years? I mean, I still can't get my head around that many years."

Dana sighed, as if it might be the last thing she'd ever do.

"That's where I get hung up too. *Why* did he have the affair? Why wasn't I enough? And did he break it off or did she? And why didn't he divorce me?"

"You've got some good questions, Mom."

"Yes, and I need to find some answers."

CHAPTER 7

Darkness closed in on Halloween day and the evening air grew chilly. Skeleton and black cat flashlights provided the light as costumed children trooped up the walkway to the Connelly's house: the inevitable Spiderman, the inimitable Casper, Punky the witch, Jolly the clown, Superman, and on they came. Ringing the doorbell. Trick or treat. In the foyer, Les greeted the kids dressed up as Darth Vadar from the original *Star Wars* movie. He traded fun banter with them and filled their bags and pumpkins with goodies that Tilly had provided in a large dish on the side table.

At the computer desk in the breakfast room, Dana Googled Claire Breen, attorney at law, in Louisville, Kentucky, and brought up one name. She read the available information: a partner at Connelly, Meyers, Breen, Woodall, Jansen and Starnes…yadda, yadda, yadda…graduate of Yale Law…top ten percent of her class…blah, blah, blah…specializes in tax law…an advocate for the poor…donates time at the *Kurbside Kitchen* in downtown Louisville…yadda…yadda…Interesting.

Dana went on reading about Claire while Les's and the children's playful remarks filtered in to her from the front of the house. She Googled the *Kurbside Kitchen* and found a recent newspaper story about this volunteer operation that benefited the city's homeless. She read every word of *The Courier Journal* article. When she finished the detailed account, she just stared at the computer screen, lost in thought. She remained lost there for a while before she hit on an idea.

* * *

Les lounged in a recliner in the hearth room the following morning, sweats and reading glasses on, working in a crossword puzzle book. Classical music played over the sound system. Through the windows behind him, clouds stacked up in the sky like gray mounds of doom. Dana walked in dressed in jeans and a sweater, and carrying her purse. She had a jacket draped over her arm. When she paused near his chair, he looked up.

"Who is Ma…Matilda Gibbons?"

"She's our maid. Tilly."

"Sergeant Gibbons is one of the answers in the crossword I'm working on. His name made me think of her. I just couldn't remember who she was exactly."

"Sergeant Gibbons in the great British mystery novel series with his dear friend Philip Bathencourt?" she asked. "Cassandra Chan's books?"

"That's a favorite series of yours, right? I wonder if he's any kin to Tilly."

It took Dana a second to get his joke, and then she smiled.

"Tilly's upstairs right now. I gladly left her to it."

Right on cue, the unseen maid revved up the vacuum cleaner, which created a not very harmonious accompaniment to the baroque piece pouring from the sound system. Les grimaced and tossed his puzzle book on the side table.

"Where are you going?" he asked. "Would you like some

company?"

"I've got a women's club meeting," she lied, "but I won't be too long." She hurried out before he could ask for a good-bye kiss.

* * *

The *Kurbside Kitchen* was a forty minute drive from Grand Oaks Village via I-71 West into downtown Louisville. It was located in an old brick storefront on West Broadway, an area of poverty and neglect and hunger, where violence was the characteristic order of the day. And the night. Faded curtains framed a pair of windows in need of a good cleaning. A crooked sign nailed over the entrance said *Kurbside Kitchen* in large broken letters that flopped this way and that way as if they were on a drunken binge. Dana cruised past in her SUV. She found a parking meter not far away, fed several quarters into it and walked back amid the scattered sidewalk rubble. She knocked on the door which swung outward in a minute, nearly banging into her. She scrambled back and stared at the man standing before her with a huge grin.

Henry Marsh, African American, had reached a ripe old age, evidenced by his crown of white hair and a face deeply lined with wrinkles. He was midsize and wore his welcome smile for everyone he met. Raised in the West End of Louisville, Henry had seen many of the city's tragedies, but had somehow managed not to let them take their desolate toll on him. He had on soiled jeans and a thread-bare shirt, and held onto the handle of a well-used broom. The delicious smell of beef stew wafted out the door.

"Don't have to knock at the *Kitchen* door, mizus," Henry boomed. "Just come on in and make yerself useful." He propped his broom against the wall and whipped out a brown, calloused hand. "Name's Henry." He shook hands with Dana enthusiastically, which was the only way old Henry did it. He was blessed with surplus energy and spread the precious stuff around as though it was a featured item in a closeout sale.

"It's so nice to meet you, Henry," she said. "My name's Dana Connelly. I'm here to see Opal Benson. She's expecting me."

"I reckoned you'd be a lookin' fer Miz Opal," he said. "We's been 'spectin' you to show up today, mizus."

Henry stepped aside, beckoning her in, and then guided her among the empty tables. Hardly the drab interior she half expected, Dana noted that the walls were painted a cheery yellow and adorned with bargain-basement pictures of charming landscapes: a little boy and a little girl sitting in a porch swing, a kitten and a puppy playing in a field of clover, birds and butterflies winging over a creek bed. She followed Henry around the steam table separating the kitchen from the dining room. Two young African American women busily prepared the day's meal at the back counter and didn't look up as they went past. Dana was impressed with the commercial equipment in the kitchen and how everything looked clean and well-organized.

The office was located behind the kitchen. Henry knocked on the door that was ajar and a woman's voice responded with a solid "Come on in." He didn't enter, but opened the door wide, stepping back and ushering Dana in with a sweeping hand gesture.

"Comp'ny's here, Miz Opal. This be Miz Dana."

Henry smiled at Dana and she thanked him before he shuffled off. She entered the small, cluttered room.

Opal Benson, African American, was in her forties. Tall and

big-boned, she wore a red shirt under gray overalls. Her clothes didn't look new, but they looked well cared for. Her tight curls were starting to turn gray and her big brown eyes appraised Dana in one astute gaze: class and money in her looks and clothes, kindness in her face. A good combination usually, but Opal had learned a long time ago not to make hasty judgments about people. That way you cut way down on the disappointment factor.

Behind an ancient, overcrowded desk, Opal reached for a stack of invoices on a nearby chair. She said, "Sit down, Dana."

Opal placed the papers on the floor on the other side of the desk and Dana sat.

"You called me at a good time," Opal said. "One of my volunteers is out for the next few weeks. Recovering from knee surgery. Now, did you tell me you'd done work like this before?"

Dana shook her head, and Opal rummaged through the desk litter for a notepad. She found one and grabbed a cheap ballpoint pen that refused to write. She pitched it at a waste basket heaping with paper debris and found another one that began cooperating after a bit of encouragement.

"You'll learn the routine quick enough," she said. "Now, how much time can you give me? That's what I need to know first."

They discussed what Opal needed and what Dana could do. And she was surprised when the woman in charge asked her why she was volunteering her time and effort to feed street people. Before Dana could decide how to answer, Opal seemed to sense her reluctance to open up and moved on. She didn't mean to question what wasn't any of her business, she explained. She was just curious about what brought good folks downtown with an urge to help out. But the fact was, Dana was there and that was all that mattered.

Later, when Opal led Dana out of her office and into the kitchen, one of the young cooks cleaned up the prep area at the back counter. At the steam table Claire stood with the other cook, where they served a hot meal to the last of the few people in a line of the homeless. The tables in the dining room were full now, but the place was quiet. These folks, a mixture of ages and races, weren't about socializing; they were about eating. Today's menu offered crunchy corn bread muffins with the delicious smelling beef stew that Dana had noticed when she arrived.

She hadn't expected to encounter Claire on her first visit to the *Kurbside Kitchen*. She paused in the doorway, trying to think of what to say now, but Opal didn't give her enough time to prepare. She bustled her along and introduced her to all three volunteers. Claire stared at Dana, surprised, while the other two gave her a friendly hello.

"Dana's taking Estelle's place while she's out on medical leave," Opal said. She focused on the two young women. "I know you girls have to get going on to school." Looking over at Claire, she added, "Dana's going to help you with kitchen clean-up today. I've got phone calls to make."

And with that she whipped around and left them to it.

* * *

While the young cooks departed for their college classes, Dana and Claire just stood there staring at each other as if they didn't know what else to do.

"Are you as surprised to see me as I am to see you?" Claire asked finally.

Dana said, "You could say I'm surprised with you, yes."

The dining room began to clear out, and Henry moved between the tables collecting used plastic bowls, cups, and spoons. He deposited them in a huge black garbage bag slung over his shoulder by the handles. While he emptied the trash and swept the floor, Dana and Claire washed the steam table and countertops. As usual, there weren't any leftovers to be dealt with. Hungry people ate until all the food was gone.

"Dana, how do you happen to be taking Estelle's place?" asked Claire.

Dana was ready for this question from her nemesis, having anticipated it ever since Opal had thrust them together so unexpectedly.

"That part's just coincidence," she replied. "I saw *The Courier's* story on the *Kurbside Kitchen* and it made me stop and think. People without homes. Without jobs. No food or decent clothes. Existing on the street. Some of them needing medication."

"They just don't have what it takes to be a part of society, a responsible, productive part," Claire explained. "They've never had a support system. Or even enough education. Or they lost their opportunities suddenly. Some of them have even been abused. Their stories are so sad."

* * *

Dana followed Claire out the front door and waited while she locked up the *Kurbside Kitchen*. They walked off down the street together toward their cars at the parking meters. A city bus, gray with red, blue and white stripes, eased to the curb and let off a passenger, a feeble African American woman who made her way along with an ancient cane. Opal had given Dana a *Kurbside Kitchen* sign that Henry had obligingly placed in the windshield of her SUV. Protection against vandalism and injury, Opal explained. Nobody living—existing—in the West End dared mess with anyone or anything connected to Miss Opal. Any such action wouldn't be conducive to continued health and welfare downtown, according to her self-appointed guardians of the neighborhood.

"One hot meal a day," Claire said, "that's all the Kitchen can do. Opal operates at the tail end of a state program. Which they keep threatening to shut off. Too many needs. Not enough funds. But with the donations she gets—that's why she spends so much time on the phone—she manages to keep going."

"I admire her dedication," Dana said as she paused beside her SUV.

The two women stared at each other. An awkward moment. Then Dana had an inspiration, but she had reservations too. On impulse, she plunged ahead.

"I don't know about you, Claire, but I could use a cup of coffee."

Claire hesitated. "Okay. There's a decent little place around the corner."

The *Forty-Second Street Bakery* was rather bleak and bare, but it was clean and not crowded in the mid-afternoon. They drank lattes at one of the tables across from the pastry-filled glass cases that lined the wall. The broad window gave an unobstructed view of the poverty and neglect. When Dana inquired, Claire described how she had become involved in feeding the homeless. Through a pro bono client at the law firm, she had learned that Opal was desperate for volunteers in the early days. Claire went on to outline herself as "a sucker for a worthy cause." But she emphasized that she received much more from helping out than she gave. It sounded simple, but probably wasn't. Doing some good just felt good, she said.

Dana managed to work their conversation around to Claire's unmarried status when she said, "We've known each other casually for years, but I don't think I've ever seen you with a date at any of the firm's social functions."

"Just call me career focused," Claire replied.

Dana nodded and stared across the table at Claire as if they'd just met. Who did this woman think she was fooling? Of course she was career focused. Look at the level of success she'd achieved: a full partner in one of Louisville's most prestigious law firms. But Claire Breen was also focused on her table companion's husband. Boy, was she ever focused on him! She'd been having an affair with him for most of his twenty-five years of married life. And, not forgetting that it still takes two to tango, his wife could've quite happily leaned over and scratched this husband-swiping witch's eyes out.

* * *

In the breakfast room that evening, cell phone clamped to her ear, Dana set the table for an informal dinner: placemats, matching napkins, silverware. She lit taper candles in a fruit and floral centerpiece and talked to her daughter. In the background through the long windows, Les filled the bird feeders and chatted with a neighbor in the cold, cloud-covered dusk.

"Tell me you didn't do this, Mom!" Gwen almost shouted. "Okay. Too late for that. Just tell me why."

"I told you yesterday, honey. I need answers to my questions. And I can't talk to your dad. Not yet."

"You really think Claire Breen will admit anything? She's a shrewd lawyer. She'll see right through you. Like you were a pane of glass."

"Yes. Maybe. I don't know. But I need to get better

acquainted with her."

Gwen scoffed. "You'll get to know only what she wants you to know."

"So I'm not a lawyer. Well, I'm not a fool either. Oh, I didn't tell you what happened last week when we went to the neurologist. On the way home your dad found Claire's card in my purse. Remember when you called and I was driving? Well, he dug out my cell phone and came across the card. He didn't recognize it."

"Not surprising, right? He *has* lost his short-term memory. And now he lives only in the moment. Well, mostly. But you lucked out there, Mom."

"I know."

"May I ask you something?"

"Sure, honey."

"You're not blaming yourself for Dad and Claire, are you? I mean, she *stole* him from you. Sort of. After all, he went along willingly with her, I assume. But that's no reflection on you. Don't start blaming yourself."

"That won't happen, Gwen. This chasm between your dad and me now, that belongs totally to him. And Claire."

* * *

A storm blew in from the West the following afternoon, swelling and battering Grand Oaks like a monsoon on a free for all. In the fitness room on the lower level of the Connelly's home, Les jogged on the treadmill wearing his head-set. Dana worked out on the stationary bike. Beyond the glass wall the fierce wind hurled the tree limbs about as if they were made of tissue paper. Half an hour later, she threw darts at the elaborate board mounted on the adjacent wall. Les observed from behind her.

She said, "I'm donating Saturday and Sunday afternoons for the next six weeks."

She took careful aim and threw. "Until the other volunteer gets back from medical leave. She had knee surgery. And Opal needs weekend help the most. Her weekdays are well covered with college students who work around their different schedules."

"Sweetheart, I don't like you...you being gone every weekend. Can't I go with you? I can help out too."

She watched him retrieve her darts. She hadn't considered that he'd want to accompany her downtown. Wouldn't that be fun? Les and his wife and his lover spending their weekend afternoon's together right up until Christmas? Would Claire want to exchange holiday gifts with her lover's wife too? Make that *former* lover. She agreed with Gwen. She didn't think that Les and Claire were seeing each other anymore. Les returned with the darts that he'd pulled from the board. He gave half of them to her.

"You want to play a game downside up? I mean, upside down?"

She tossed a dart underhand and missed the bull's eye. "I have a suggestion about my volunteer project. The two afternoons I'm gone, you could go over to the East End Center. They have crafts and games. And they serve lunch. They even take day trips. A lot of retired people go over there. Last week they made bird houses and took—."

"I don't want to build a damn bird house!" Les shouted. "The East End Center's an adult day care. For people losing their minds. You think I need that?"

Not yet.

"You're not—" She stopped and started over. "You're accustomed to being busy during the day. I just thought—"

"I had to retire early, Dana. Much too early. But I'm trying to accept that. You know what the best part of being retired is? Spending my days with you."

She swung away from her husband suddenly. She didn't want him to read her expression. All she'd ever wanted was to spend her days with him. Until Claire. She turned and let a dart go for the board as if she was throwing a hand grenade at an enemy target. It landed in the outer bull's eye ring. Les gave her a strange look before throwing his dart and hitting the next inner ring. The game continued in silence as dart after dart smacked the board. She pulled them free this time. He watched her bring the darts back and give half of them to him.

He said, "Dana, why don't we have sex anymore?"

She cut loose with her next dart. It barely lodged into the edge of the board. She stared when it tipped over and dropped to the floor as if the dart had lost all of its pizzazz. Just like their romantic life. He stared at her. The dart game was all of a sudden forgotten. Seconds ticked away.

"I can't explain right now," she said.

"Do you still love me? Do you even want a man who can't remember what he had for lunch minutes after he eats? I can leave you know. You don't have to put up with me this way."

She exhaled a jagged breath. "Do you want to leave?" He shook his head.

"Who—if you left, *where* would you go?"

"I don't know. But if that's what you want, I'll go."

He waited and she didn't say anything. They just stood there looking at each other like two people who didn't know who they were, let alone what they wanted.

At last he said, "I think I yelled at you a minute ago. I'm sorry."

In an unexpected surge of sympathy for him, she said, "I know."

"Forgive me?"

She watched him some more. She could forgive him for anything. Except Claire.

CHAPTER 8

Upstairs in the master suite the next morning, Dana slept nestled down under the covers like a bear curled up in its den, hibernating for the winter. Les bustled noisily out of his closet wearing suit pants and buttoning his dress shirt. She roused gradually and peeked out at him, ready to play the grouchy bear role for being wakened.

"Look at the time!" he said, flustered. "I'm late for the office!"

Dana almost growled at him. She groaned instead. A pitiful murmur in her throat. Yesterday, he had a decent grip on reality. Today, he treaded hopelessly through Never-Never Land. Dementia was nothing if not a roller-coaster ride, especially for the caregiver, and she didn't know how much longer she could hang on through the ups and downs of his devastating ailment. *There will be good days and some days won't be so good,* she reminded herself.

"Les, no. You don't go into the office anymore. You retired. In October."

He paused at the foot of the bed. "How could I forget that? What month is this?"

"November."

"Why did I retire?"

The handset on the bedside table sang a merry tune and she ignored it. She pulled the covers over her head again as he came around the bed, checked for the caller, and then answered.

"Hello, Aunt Nettie…Yes, I'm doing well, thank you…Yes, just fine."

Aunt Nettie reclined on a lounger in her sunroom in full regalia—an orange print muumuu the size of a tarpaulin draping her bulk, with a ballast of chunky black jewelry to accessorize. Ears. Neck. Wrists. Her face was moldy with make-up. She stroked her tiny pedigree dog, Booboo.

"You know what *fine* stands for, don't you?" she asked. "Frustrated. Insecure. Neurotic. And emotional." She cackled like an old witch. "Read that somewhere."

Les didn't bother to make a comment, but dropped the phone on the bed next to Dana's pillow. "It's for you," he said, heading back to his closet.

She dredged up a dramatic sigh while fumbling for the phone. She got it to her ear eventually. "Morning, whoever you are."

"We really need to talk about Christmas, my dear," Aunt Nettie informed her.

"You're having the family this year as usual, aren't you?"

Dana stifled a banshee scream. "I don't think so."

"Why ever not?"

She tried to think up an unassailable excuse as Les backed out of his closet, still dressed in his suit pants, but with his shirt completely unbuttoned now. He came over to the bed while her sleepy brain worked on a plausible reason why she couldn't have the extended family over for the holidays this year.

"Dana, sweetheart, excuse me. Why am I dressed like this?"

She gritted her teeth and fought down another scream. Aunt Nettie on a good day was an ordeal. Les, with dementia now, was a trial most of the time (no lawyer pun intended), but both of them at once was like turning a somersault without using your hands. Only an experienced acrobat could do it.

"Just a minute, Aunt Nettie," Dana said into the phone and laid it on the blankets.

"Les, why don't you put on your corduroys. Think warm and comfy around the house."

He nodded and strode away as she grabbed the phone again. "Aunt Nettie, I've got a little too much going on right now to do Christmas."

"How difficult can it be? Everybody brings a dish."

"Sounds great. Why don't you be our hostess this year?"

* * *

Les sat at the desk in his study later that morning, playing a word game on the computer. The phone jingled and he reached over for it.

"Hello…What'd you say, Marty?...I left you a message yesterday about golf?... Must've been…Sure, this afternoon sounds good. I think Dana's got some charity project or the other. You don't think it's too cold to play?" He laughed. "Right. It's never too hot or too cold on the golf course…Exactly."

Les glanced up when Dana paused out in the foyer with her purse. "I'm off."

He tapped his cheek for a kiss. She waved good-bye and pretended to miss his gesture. She hurried off to the garage. He spoke into the phone.

"What did you say, Marty?...Oh, she did. Tell Joan I'll mention it to Dana. And we'll plan it for another time."

He reached for a notepad beside the computer and jotted on

it: JOAN WANTS A FOURSOME FOR GOLF SOON.

* * *

That afternoon a chilly wind swept like a fury along the downtown streets and between the towering old buildings. Cloud swirls parted, offering quick glimpses of a sun that couldn't quite heat up the day. Inside the *Kurbside Kitchen,* the homeless line extended from the front door around the dining room walls to the steam table. Dana and Claire served burgers and brown beans with macaroni and cheese. No one in the long line spoke a word. They were all focused on their only meal of the day.

Later, when the homeless began leaving, Henry, huge trash bag over his shoulder, did the clean-up at the emptying tables. Behind the steam table, Claire paused to catch her breath, pushing damp hair away from her face. Dana wiped her hands on a towel and watched a young couple at a table with a toddler.

"How in God's name do you live on the street with a young child?" asked Dana.

Claire said, "I can't imagine."

"I told Opal to put Les and me on her donations list. These people break my heart. How did they wind up like this? I know you told me a little about that. But some of them seem as if they have potential. How did they fall so far?"

"We're seeing more families here now. Jobless and homeless go hand in hand sometimes. With no support. No resources. Not enough education. No opportunities. Without any of that, it's hard to have ambition. Or self-confidence. I think they just don't know *how* to have a life."

Dana and Claire watched as more of the homeless finished

eating, got up and left.

"Some of these people," Claire went on, "have lost their jobs and homes, and a portion of their minds too. They need their meds every day just to handle the basics. I don't understand most of these people, but I don't know what circumstances led them to this end. If nothing else, helping out here has taught me not to make judgments."

Dana stared at Claire as they began the clean-up process. She hated to admit it, but this woman who wanted to take Les away from her wasn't all bad. Well, of course not. Was anyone *all* bad? For example, how many felons had Les defended—or declined to defend—who had no regard for other people, but were passionate about their pets? As for Claire, for one minute—just for one minute—Dana almost wished they could be friends.

No! No! No! She took that back. How could she even think such a thing? She could *never* be friends with this woman.

Later, Henry swept up across the room while Dana and Claire sat at a table by the front windows with cups of hot tea.

Dana said, "Do you have time to talk to Les when he calls the office? Since he retired, he enjoys chatting up whichever partner can give him a few minutes."

Claire considered her table companion, considered what might lie behind the question. "Les misses his job, Dana. It was his life."

Dana frowned. "Not quite. Are the partners going to replace him?"

"We're sharing his workload right now. We'll have to make a decision about that after the holidays."

* * *

Dana's SUV wheeled into the driveway and the garage door glided up. She pulled inside and turned off the ignition. But she didn't close the door and get out yet. She was back from her afternoon at the *Kurbside Kitchen* and her little chat with Claire over tea. She took Claire's anniversary card from her purse, removed it from the envelope and opened it. She stared at the date below the handwritten note—July 2014.

She stared and remembered.

* * *

At the Emerald Coast Resort Hotel in Naples on Florida's southern Gulf Coast, seagulls winged low over the clear green water and pristine white beach. Pleasure boats drifted past with leaping dolphins in their wake. High on one of the hotel balconies, Dana and Les danced in a loving embrace to romantic music wafting out through the open glass doors. They tenderly kissed and he slipped the strap of her gown over her shoulder. He pressed a kiss there. And another. He kissed her neck. They moved inside and he lowered the other strap. He lovingly kissed the bare spot.

* * *

Dana came back to the present, abruptly. She closed the card and slipped it back into the envelope and down into her purse. Her cell phone rang and she pulled it out and checked the caller ID.

"Hi, Gwen."

"I've just got a few minutes between classes, but I wanted to check on you."

Dana said, "Seventeen years ago. Your dad started seeing

Claire just one month after our second honeymoon vacation. How could he do that?"

"You're asking *me* that question?"

"Not really. I'm asking myself."

"So, Mom, when you figure it out…"

* * *

Two days later Dana sat down at the computer desk in the breakfast room with her morning cup of coffee. She picked up her glasses by the computer, slid them on and reached for the mouse. She spotted the note Les had written and shoved aside while he talked to Joan's husband Marty. She grabbed it instead. She glanced up when Les strolled in slipping on a jacket over his sweats.

"Sweetheart, you want to go for a jog with me?" he asked. "When you finish checking your…your e-mails?"

Dana said, "Tell me about this note."

Les took the notepaper she offered him, feeling in his pockets for his glasses and coming up without them. She jerked the note back and read it to him.

"Joan wants a foursome for golf ASAP."

"Sounds pretty straightforward to me."

"Yes, but when did you write this? Can you recall?"

Les looked blank. He stared at the note in her hand. Dana waited impatiently, tapping her foot. Then she gave up and tried to help.

"You played golf with Marty on Saturday."

"I did?"

"You were on the phone with him when I left for the *Kurbside Kitchen*."

"Okay. Then he must've told me that Joan wanted the four

of us to play."

"Can you remember what you told Marty?" She crossed her fingers.

"I guess I said that you couldn't play on weekends for a while…because of your…your…what is it? I can't think of the word."

Les focused hard and Dana let him chase around after his word for a bit. Finally, his brain kicked in and he found it. "Charity! Your charity thing in the afternoons. Is that right, sweetheart?"

She nodded absently as she removed her glasses and stood up with her coffee mug. She wandered off with Joan on her mind. She owed her friend an explanation now. Not that Joan would agree. She was like that. Tolerant. Understanding. Quick. Wise. But still, Joan was bound to wonder why her closest friend had said no to their women's club Christmas undertaking, and then immediately jumped into another commitment that would last right up to the big holiday.

When Dana entered the kitchen later with her empty coffee mug, Les was at the fridge checking out the breakfast possibilities and talking on the mobile phone.

"You know how much I love the law, son, but even I know the last thing the world needs is another lawyer…Graham, son, there must be something that you're passionate about…yes, but besides Leah…and fishing."

Dana opened the dishwasher, found a place for her mug and wedged it between a glass and a bowl. Les finished his phone call and walked over, explaining that Graham was on his way to pick him up for breakfast and a trip to the local ice skating rink. As soon as they left, she called Joan before her day got underway, inviting her over for brunch. And then she got busy making a spinach omelet, crisp bacon, hashbrowns, and a bowl of fresh fruit. Lastly, she turned her attention to setting the table in the breakfast room: lace tablecloth, antique dishes and candlelight. That should do it. Or was she overdoing it? Joan would figure it out in a heartbeat.

Toward the end of their brunch, Dana watched Joan across the table spooning fruit salad from a large bowl into her dish. Orange slices and kiwis went on top of melon cubes and strawberries.

"Why don't I have a good feeling about this?" asked Joan. "Your grandmother's dishes. The lace. The candles. This has all been so lovely, but something else is going on here, my sweet."

"If you only knew."

"So tell me already. The suspense is too much."

Suddenly, Dana wanted to stall, not tell. She was losing her nerve. Was she doing the right thing here? She was about to knock her best friend's socks off too. Wasn't that at least a little unfair? Not to mention that she would be confiding the hideous truth about her twenty-five year happy marriage, even to Joan. Whoever said that the wife always knows was *so* wrong. She still had trouble believing that Les had spent seventeen years of their married life with her—and Claire.

"I owe you an explanation," she began, "about my weekend project downtown. You've probably wondered about it after I told you that I couldn't handle our women's club Christmas affair."

"You don't owe me any explanation. I did wonder what was up after Marty said that you couldn't play the golf foursome for a while because you had a volunteer commitment. I knew there was more to the story, but..." She grinned. "Les wasn't supposed to mention that, was he?"

Dana jumped up. "You want more coffee?"

Not waiting for an answer, she grabbed both of their cups

and went over to the coffeemaker on the kitchen counter for refills. She came carefully back with them and sat down. She watched Joan playing in her fruit salad now, spooning blueberries around.

"Joan, what would you do if you woke up tomorrow and discovered that the world as you know it has come to an end?"

Her old friend stared at her for a minute. Then she said, "You're not serious?"

"When I told you I couldn't do the Christmas project this year, I didn't know that I'd be volunteering elsewhere. This undertaking began as a means to an end."

Fifteen minutes later Joan gazed at Dana across the table in wretched disbelief. At last, she got up and paced around the breakfast room and through the kitchen, over to the fireplace in the hearth room and back. She dropped into her chair looking sick.

"I've got something to tell you, Dana. Oh, dear God, why didn't I...?" She stopped and started over. "I should've... I...Well, anyway, I didn't. So...let's see...it was five years ago. No. Six years ago. Remember that convention I went to with Marty in Las Vegas? Wives aren't usually invited to corporate gatherings, you know, but this one had a social calendar too."

* * *

APRIL 2008

The *Venetian* stood in all of its resplendent glory on the Las Vegas strip beneath a vast, cloudless evening sky. In the winding Grand Canal out in front of the hotel, Joan and Marty rode side by side in a gondola moving toward the main entrance. The gondolier stood on an elevated platform behind them, guiding the boat with a long paddle and singing a soft Italian ballad in his clear baritone. He finished the song as he stopped the gondola and helped his passengers step out near the front door. Marty tipped him nicely and the two men chatted for a minute while Joan headed on inside out of the heat.

In the cool, fragrant lobby, at the registration desk, Les sat down his overnight bag and stepped up to the counter. Claire walked up from the direction of the casino and paused beside him. They exchanged smiles and she laid her hand briefly on his arm. Just as she removed her hand, Joan entered and saw them. She paused, surprised. She took a step toward them, but changed her mind about going over. Quickly, she swung around and went back outside.

* * *

NOVEMBER 2014

"Why didn't you go on over and speak to them?" Dana asked.

"I honestly don't know. I think—I know—I thought the worst. At first. Then I realized that she didn't have any luggage. He did but she didn't. So I gave them the benefit of the doubt. They didn't seem to be together. It looked as though they just ran into each other. So during my stay there with Marty, I talked myself out of any suspicion. Les is...he...I just didn't think that he would...anyway, I knew Les didn't travel often for his clients. But when he did, he sometimes went with another partner. And I really didn't see anything more than coworker familiarity with Claire. So I decided that they were there on business. End of story."

"Did you see them together at other times?"

"No, but Marty and I left the next morning. Oh, sweetie, I'm *so* sorry."

"Gwen said that in seventeen years, somebody would've seen something. Joan, think about the longevity."

"I know. So many years and he's been with you all that time. He loves you, Dana, that's why. Absolutely."

"So Claire was what? Just some…some extra sex along the way? The thrill of the forbidden fruit? For all that time?"

Dana and Joan stared at each other. Joan couldn't say the words, but at last Dana said them for her. "You think Les loves Claire too, don't you?"

And now Dana understood why Claire had never found a romantic partner. She'd always wondered about that. A woman so brilliant and beautiful. She hadn't found anyone because she already had someone. Someone who belonged to her, to Dana. Someone Claire had no right to. Someone who didn't say no but should have.

* * *

A few evenings later, Dana entered the house from the garage carrying a bag of groceries. In the kitchen she placed it on the counter with her purse. Les called out to her from his study.

"Dana, sweetheart, can you come in here?"

She frowned. What now? She'd been gone from the house for less than an hour. Just a brief trip to the market. How much trouble could he get into in that length of time?

When she walked into the study, he sat at the desk, going through the drawers, frantic.

A thick book lay beside the computer. She glanced at the title: *Judicial Opinions in Case Law*.

"I've lost my…my…my...glasses!"

"Take a deep breath, Les. Calm down. I'll check in the hearth room. They probably slipped down between the cushions in the recliner."

She came back shaking her head. "But they aren't lost. They're here somewhere. Did you check up in the bedroom?"

"Have I been up there since I got up this morning?"

She just got home. She didn't know. And didn't bother with such an obvious answer. She took off into the foyer and up the staircase. He sat there gazing after her as if he wasn't sure what to do next. Up in the master suite, she froze in the doorway and stared. It took a minute for her to grasp the situation. Then she yelled down to him.

"Les, come up here!"

His footsteps sounded on the stairs right away. When he strode up behind her, his expression was calmer.

"Did you find my glasses?"

"Les, why are you packing?"

He peered over her shoulder at the piece of his luggage open on their kingsize bed with several pairs of khakis and shirts folded inside.

"Did I do that?"

"Where are you going?"

"I…I don't…let's see…I think Pete called and asked me to look up a case law ruling for him. Someone borrowed his favorite book and he can't find the ruling he wants." Les checked his pockets. "I wrote down the ruling so I could call him back and give him the correct one for his case." He pulled a slip of paper from his pocket and gestured at his luggage. Dana watched him. "I should unpack, shouldn't I?"

"Not if you're leaving."

"Where am I going?"

She ignored him and strolled over to her closet. She was

beyond caring whether he stayed or went now. As for where he was going? To Claire, of course. Where else would he go? She disregarded a voice inside of her saying—*what about Graham and his friends on the boat? You know those guys. They could always make room for one more.*

Les unpacked his suitcase and came across his reading glasses in a zippered side pocket. Dana stepped out of her closet slipping on her house shoes. He held his glasses up, grinning. She sighed and shook her head. He closed his luggage and put it away in his closet. In his study a few minutes later, he ended a phone call with Pete and returned his case law book to its place on the wall shelf. Upstairs in the bedroom, she carried a piece of luggage out of her closet and opened it on the bed. The phone by the bed jingled and she checked the caller ID and answered.

"Hi, Joan."

"Is this a good time? I'm not interrupting dinner?"

"No."

"How are you doing, sweetie?"

"I'm packing." She flopped on the bed by her empty suitcase. "Les was getting ready to leave a few minutes ago, but he got sidetracked. Now he's not going. But I've decided that two can play this leaving game."

"I know you've thought this through."

"Well…I…what do you think?"

"I think, if I were you, I wouldn't leave. Unless you don't care that Les might invite Claire to move in."

Dana sat up with a start. Why hadn't she thought of that? "She can have him, but not in my house!"

"That's my girl!"

Dana laughed. "Oh, I get it now. Aren't you just Miss Clever. I guess that psychology class you took in college was worth something after all."

Joan laughed. "You would've thought of it on your own soon enough."

When Dana hung up from her phone call, she whisked her luggage back to the closet. What would she do without Joan and her calm wisdom? She needed to cultivate some of that on her own.

CHAPTER 9

Dana padded into the smoky kitchen in her nightgown the next morning, half asleep still, and aiming for the coffeemaker. Les threw open the windows in the breakfast room, letting in the chilly air but drawing out the heavy smoke. Slowly. The table was set with placemats and matching napkins. Classical music drifted from the sound system. The November sky was gloomy with rain clouds. She filled a coffee mug and blew and sipped while he explained the smoke.

"I burned the first batch of French toast," he said, going back to the cook top. "But this batch is perfect." He grabbed the pancake turner and ladled French toast from a skillet onto two plates. "What kind of syrup do you want?" He carried the plates over to the table, and then went to the fridge and opened the door. He pulled out several syrup bottles. "We've got blueberry, strawberry and maple."

Later, sated and lazy, they lingered at the table over second cups of coffee.

"Can't start the day without that caffeine fix," he said with a laugh. "I called Gwenie earlier. I wanted to catch her before her first class."

Dana didn't comment. She gazed past him out the closed

windows at the trees on the back lawn, their bare limbs shifting in a sudden gust of wind.

"I don't think she wanted to talk to me," he went on. "Said she was already studying hard for her finals coming up. I think Gwen's angry with me about something."

Dana rose and carried their empty plates over to the dishwasher. She didn't know whether Les could read anything in her face or not, but she didn't want to take a chance that he might. If he thought that she knew what was going on with their daughter, he would insist on an explanation.

Les said, "When is Thanksgiving?"

"Two weeks."

"Are the kids coming over?"

"Just the five of us for turkey and football."

"Five? Oh, yes. Graham's friend. What's her name?...Leah. That's right. Nice young lady. Isn't she still in college? Maybe she'll influence Graham to go back and finish his education."

Dana cleared the table and loaded the dishwasher, hoping that Les was right, but she had to admit that their son's continuing education hadn't been a chief concern in recent weeks. Actually, she hadn't even given it a thought. She trusted Graham to make the right decisions for his future, but if he wanted more parental input—which she seriously doubted—he knew that their advice was no more than a visit or a phone call away. More to the point—or should she say, closer to the truth?—she was so consumed with Les's lengthy unfaithfulness via Claire Breen that she could barely function. And just how long did she think she could go on this way? Pretending? She still wasn't ready to confront her husband with her knowledge of his affair. But what about having it out with Claire? Was she ready for that?

Yes!

But it was almost two more weeks before the right opportunity presented itself. And even then, the situation didn't play out quite the way she'd planned.

* * *

Sooty clouds piled up over downtown Louisville, turning the afternoon sky into a smoky darkness. At the *Kurbside Kitchen* Christmas lights twinkled in the gloom. Inside, amid a festive atmosphere of bargain decorations and recorded music, homeless folks jammed the dining room. Behind the steam table, Dana and Claire took a break after serving beef and potato hash with a side of green beans and wheat rolls. They sipped hot tea from chipped mugs and watched Opal and Henry move from table to table, giving out candy bars tied with red ribbons. Opal had asked everyone to stay after the *Kitchen* closed one day last week to help her accomplish this task, although Claire didn't stay because of a late courtroom appearance that she hadn't been able to reschedule.

At one table an old man held onto his candy bar almost reverently and just stared at it. An elderly woman sniffed her bar with a toothless grin. A middle-aged woman clawed her wrapper and devoured her chocolate as if she was afraid someone might try to take it away. A young man looked at his candy bar in disbelief before clutching it to his chest and sighing. Treats such as candy happened rarely in Opal's food budget.

"Paddy and Martina thanked me personally for their lunch," Dana said.

"Some of them will give you something this time of year," Claire replied. "A coin they found or a trinket."

Dana sat down her mug. "You know what's so wrong with

this scene? When these people finish eating, they still have to go back out in the street in the terrible cold."

Late that afternoon rain beat down in a torrent and threatened to turn into snow.

In front of the *Kitchen,* umbrella up, Dana dashed for her SUV at a parking meter down the street. Claire hurried along right behind her with her umbrella, splashing water on both of them. Suddenly, she stopped. Dana kept going.

"I totally forgot," Claire said. "My car's being serviced. They didn't get to it yesterday. So I took a cab down here. I'll go back and—"

"Come on," Dana called back to her, "I'll take you home."

They settled into Dana's Volvo and folded their wet umbrellas on the floor.

"Where do you live, Claire?"

"In one of those ancient relics in the Highlands area," she replied. "On Trevillian Way. Do you know it?"

Dana thought for a minute and shook her head. "From out in Grand Oaks, I come into downtown on I-71."

Claire said, "Just go on down Broadway until it ends at Baxter Avenue. At Cave Hill Cemetery, you turn right. That's Baxter. Trevillian turns off Baxter, but on down a little further."

Dana followed rain-slick Broadway in moderate traffic and focused on her driving. Claire gazed out the passenger's window at the city's mix of old and new buildings. The windshield wipers slapped out the only sound. The silence between the two women stretched out. Seconds ticked into minutes. The quiet grew awkward. Tension mounted, unexpectedly. Dana worked on how she wanted to begin. She was making headway when Claire beat her to the punch.

"You know, don't you?"

Dana gripped the steering wheel as if it were a life-preserver and she was a drowning swimmer. She dragged in a deep breath, eased off the accelerator. She couldn't look at Claire. Not even a glance.

"Oh, the big debate," Claire said. "Should I play games here or should I be straight? Correct me if I'm wrong—although I know I'm not—I'm the reason you're volunteering at the *Kitchen*. It was too much of a coincidence that you just showed up."

"You're very good. My daughter warned me how shrewd you are."

"Did Les tell you about us?"

"I don't think how I found out is any of your concern."

"So he didn't tell you. In court, the first rule a litigator applies—a good litigator and I'm one of the best—never ask your witness a question on cross if you don't already know the answer."

The rain subsided all of a sudden and the threat of snow disappeared without a trace, but the clouds hung around like a fervent promise. The last few raindrops bounced off the windshield. The glass dried and Dana shut off the wipers.

"Will you tell me about you and Les?" she asked.

Claire gave that some thought. "I suppose I owe you that much."

* * *

It was a snowy January morning in 1997, Claire began. On the 4th floor of the Oaks office building in Grand Oaks Village, she walked up to a glass door embossed with two names—Connelly and Meyers. She looked like a million dollars in a gray business suit, not a hair out of place, and her make-up perfectly applied. She was nervous but didn't let it show. She had studied and worked so hard for this opportunity. A short time later she sat in a conference room across from Les and Pete at a long table polished to such a high gloss that she could see her reflection in the shine. Classic reproductions adorned the walls and a pair of broad windows overlooked a small park. She had done her homework on this tiny law firm and knew that they were first class and rising quickly to the top of the legal heap. Exactly where she wanted to be. Except she got a lot more than she bargained for at the interview.

Coffee cups sat on the table in front of them. Pete studied her résumé while Les and Claire gazed at each other. Pete was oblivious as she noted Les's wedding ring and he checked the third finger of her left hand. No ring. Suddenly, they were looking everywhere but at each other.

"We met in January, seventeen years ago," Claire said, "when Les and Pete hired me. And Les and I were attracted to each other from the moment we met. Which completely threw me. I didn't think anyone was more career oriented that I was. Love was the last thing on my mind then. Anyway, we fought our feelings. Hard."

Les and Claire went through their daily office routines, with and without clients, acknowledging each other, but not much more. Two ships passing in the night. They met in the hallway, lugging briefcases heavy with work, and exchanged benign nods and smiles. They met in the lounge at the coffeemaker and discussed cases, legal documents in hand, expressions set in strictly business mode. They spent three months avoiding the inevitable. All to no avail. Finally, they simply couldn't resist the pull of their mutual attraction any longer.

Claire said, "It actually happened quite by accident. We ran into each other at the East End Mall."

On an April afternoon amid the bustling shoppers along the

main corridor, Les fumbled with several packages. He was about to drop one when Claire came by carrying two shopping bags. She rearranged purchases into one bag and offered him the use of the other one. After he accepted and loaded up, he offered to buy her a cup of coffee. She agreed and they adjourned to the mall coffee shop. And to this day she didn't understand, nor did he, why they hadn't encountered anyone who knew one or the other of them. Just random luck was the only explanation. So they drank cappuccinos. They talked and laughed. Time passed and still they had more to say, more to laugh about. Relaxed and content, they whiled away the hours together, connecting so naturally that they didn't realize what was happening. But the bond was established and wouldn't go away.

"Following that April at the mall," Claire went on, "we went back to being just colleagues at the office. We were still trying not to act on how we felt about each other. But at last, in June, we had to work on a case together. After that we...well, we..."

"Committed adultery," Dana supplied when Claire didn't.

Dana made a right turn off Broadway onto Baxter Avenue and drove past Cave Hill Cemetery on the left, fighting the urge to stop and let Claire out at the old burial site. In Dana's mind that was what the other woman in the car with her deserved. *The other woman.* How apropos. She felt as if she could quite gladly bury her alive.

"I certainly don't excuse Les," she said, "but why didn't you have any further reservations about his being married?"

"Believe it or not, I still did. We both did. We really tried *not* to fall in love. Even when it was too late."

"Oh, come on, Claire. Do I look *that* gullible?" Claire passed on that one and Dana continued. "So why didn't Les divorce me?"

"I knew before he even told me—in the beginning, by the way—that he'd never leave his family. And I didn't want him to. Oh, I did at first. Until I realized that he's not the kind of man who could build a separate happiness out of his family's pain."

"Do you understand this…well…this…triangle?"

"No more than you do. But there it is. I made my choice seventeen years ago, as difficult as it was. I don't have any regrets."

"How did you and Les…how did you manage to get together? Les brought work home. He seldom stayed late at the office. And he didn't travel much. How did you…? How did you…?"

"See each other privately? Seldom. He seldom stayed late. You're right. But he stayed. He didn't travel much. But he travelled."

"So you did meet him in Las Vegas? That wasn't coincidence?"

Claire glanced over at Dana, wondering, but only for an instant. "Someone you know saw us there. Probably when we checked in. We didn't go places together. Too much risk. Most of our clients go to Vegas. But we had a business conference there."

"I think I recall that."

"Oh, here's Trevillian Way coming up. Get ready to make a left turn."

Trevillian Way was an historic, high-end, hilly street lit by an array of Christmas displays gleaming brilliantly in the murky afternoon. Claire pointed out her house, and Dana turned in and stopped along the steep driveway.

"Thank you for bringing me home," Claire said. "Will you come in for a drink?"

When Dana hesitated, she said, "Come on, we're not finished with this conversation."

Dana tried to cover her surprise, but she was curious about what else Claire had to say. She followed the hated woman out of the SUV and up a row of elevated steps. A gorgeous wreath decorated the front door. In the foyer they removed their coats and hooked them on an elaborate coat tree. The living room/dining room combo was an eclectic mix that leaned toward the contemporary. Claire put away her keys and dropped her purse on a chair. At the fireplace across the room, she pressed a button on the side and gas logs blazed to life in the stone hearth. She turned on the Christmas tree nearby while Dana gazed around. She laid her purse on a side table.

"Would you care for coffee? Or wine?" asked her hostess as she walked over to the bar along the adjacent wall.

Dana followed her slowly. "White wine, if you have it."

Claire filled two slender wine glasses and stood at the bar with hers. She watched her guest stroll around, sipping her drink and admiring the artwork.

"So where do we go from here?" Claire asked in a minute.

Dana swung around and stared at her. She tried to read her face and couldn't. The inscrutable attorney persona. "I don't understand."

"Have you and Les talked about this?"

Dana hesitated. "Not yet." She took another sip of her wine. "Are you still seeing my husband?"

Claire smiled at the unmistakable message. "Les ended our...association when he decided to leave the firm. I haven't seen him since the retirement party."

She watched Dana at the bookcases, looking over the first editions and the Japanese figurines. "I don't know why I've told you all this. Must be some guilt in there somewhere." She laughed.

Dana glanced over at her, clearly not convinced or amused. "Will you tell me why Les ended the affair?"

"Surely you know. Les realized that he can't rely on his memory now. He was afraid you'd find out about us, because of something he said or did. The bottom line here is this: because of his dementia, Les had to make a choice. He chose you. And his kids."

Dana faced Claire. Examined her. Loathed her. And she didn't try to hide it.

Claire, unperturbed, finished her wine and turned away to get more. "Would you like a refill?"

"No, thank you."

"I wanted a child," Claire continued while replenishing her own glass. "Let me rephrase that, as we lawyers often say. I wanted *Les's* child. He wouldn't agree. I almost ended our relationship over that. I thought he was being quite selfish. I thought about going off the pill—this was a number of years ago, of course." She turned with her fresh drink. "Now I'm not willing to give him up without a fight."

"You've lost me again."

"I've just been giving Les some time since we stopped seeing each other. I haven't even begun to fight for him." She laughed again. Was the wine affecting her?

"I guess I shouldn't be telling you this." Yes, the wine was taking affect. "But it's just that simple."

"That's where you're wrong, Claire. It's anything but simple. Especially now. Les no longer has any short-term memory. Well, hardly any. Translation—he doesn't have much of a life, apart from his everyday routine. Do you have any idea what his future holds? He has good and bad days now. Eventually, there won't be any good ones, and the bad ones will become horrible."

"I can take care of him. I *want* to take care of him."

"Even when he eventually forgets what a bathroom's for?"

Claire leaned against the back of the bar, facing Dana with her practiced attorney face again—inscrutable.

"Les's situation will never be pretty," Dana went on.

Claire said, "For richer, for poorer. In sickness and in health. The only reason I didn't exchange those vows with Les is because you got there first."

Dana's smile spread across her face. "And that makes me the winner!"

Triumphantly, she walked over and picked up her purse en route to the bar. "Thank you for the hospitality. And for being so straight with me."

"I don't plan to live the rest of my life without Les. As I said, I'm willing to fight for him. Maybe you should consider that a warning."

Dana started to place her half-full glass on the shiny surface of the bar. Instead, she smiled suddenly, wickedly. "And you know that old maxim, Claire. Forewarned is forearmed."

And with that she threw her remaining wine in Claire's startled face. Dana let the glass fall on the carpet and stalked out to the foyer for her coat. In a minute the front door slammed behind her.

CHAPTER 10

That evening Dana met Gwen at *Grounded,* the favorite student hangout around the corner from the University of Louisville campus on Third Street. Cups of coffee sat on the table in front of them, untouched. Only a few students occupied the other tables; the coffeehouse wasn't busy tonight.

"Claire Breen's a bitch, Mom."

"Don't, honey," Dana said. "Words like that only make *you* sound bad."

"I know. I'm sorry. But I'm angry. So what if Claire helps out at a soup kitchen. And so what if she does some pro bono work for her clients. While she and my dad…"

The tears hit Gwen's eyes unbidden and spilled down her face unchecked. Dana reached over and squeezed her hand. Gwen swiped at her face with the back of her hand while her mother took a tissue from her purse. She passed it across the table and her daughter cleaned off her cheeks.

"This is the first time I've cried about Dad."

"About time."

Gwen laughed and crumpled the tissue in her lap.

"I regret involving you in this," Dana added. "I haven't told Graham. I don't know why. I told you; I should tell him too."

"I'm working through it," Gwen said, nodding. "I love Dad so much. Nothing he can say or do will ever change that. He's a wonderful father. I guess he just couldn't help being stupid."

"He could help it. Absolutely. And Claire could have too."

Gwen blew on her coffee and drank some. She played with her cup, twisting it this way and that way on the table.

"Dad's been living this lie for seventeen years. How does he do that?"

"I don't know, honey. But he does it very well."

"Aren't lawyers supposed to be the world's best liars or something?"

"The world's best strategists."

"Same thing."

They both laughed, and then they sat in silence for a minute.

"You know what?" Dana said. "I haven't done any Christmas shopping."

Gwen perked up. "Well, you'd better get busy. Want some help?"

* * *

Snow fell lightly on Christmas afternoon during the extended family's gathering at Aunt Nettie's mansion in Beaumont Reserve. Christmas lights blazed outdoors and cars filled the circular driveway. Inside, a gigantic tree decorated the dining room where the traditional dinner took place up and down the length of the elegant table. A pair of maids in red and white uniforms came and went while Aunt Nettie presided over the elaborate occasion. She wore a holiday muumuu as bright as the season itself, with sparkling jewelry hanging from her ears, her neck, her wrists like ornaments from the tree. Every gesture she made caused a sleigh bell jingle around the room.

"I got A's on all of my finals," Gwen announced.

Aunt Nettie lifted her heavy wine goblet. Jingle. Jingle. "Here's to our future pediatrician!"

The group joined in the toast, and then Graham smiled at Leah seated beside him before he spoke to the gathering.

"I sure can't top Gwenie's news, but I know Dad for one's going to like what I've got to say." He focused on Dana. "You too, Mom."

Dana and Les beamed at their son.

"You're going back to school!" Les said.

"Not yet, Dad, but I've got a job. A *real* job, as you'd say. At Estes Contracting. They're an old client of your firm."

"An old *big* client," Les replied. "You know that they're one of the area's largest commercial contractors."

"Dad, Bob Estes keeps one of his cabin cruisers at the marina," Graham went on. "And we've been talking when he comes and takes her out. I'm interested in what he does. The actual work."

"That's what you want to do, son?" asked Les. "Hard, physical labor?"

"I want to try it, Dad. I like being outdoors, for one thing. I like physical work too. That doesn't mean I won't be using my brain. And, maybe, down the road, I'll decide to switch over to administration. I can almost say for sure that I will. I want to learn every aspect of his work. So I'll finish school. Just not right away."

"To our future contractor!" Aunt Nettie cried, raising her glass again in a salute and she jingled away. The gang joined in while snow floated down and piled up outside the tall windows.

In the hearth room later, family members talked and laughed as they opened gifts around a magnificent tree. Logs flamed in the fireplace and Aunt Nettie's Yoranian terrier, Booboo, delighted in the presents' exchange, romping and playing among the wrappings and ribbons. As the day's excitement wound down, Aunt Nettie rested on a lounger by the fireside with Booboo, both of them weary after all the festivities. Her company departed in pairs and small groups, gifts in tow and bundled up for the weather. Gwen left with Graham and Leah while Dana sat on the floor next to her aunt, organizing hers and Les's presents. Aunt Nettie observed Les roaming restlessly about the large room after his children had gone. He paused by his wife.

"Dana, sweetheart, everyone's going. Do you…you know where our coats are?"

"The maid will bring them when we're ready to go, Les."

"Are we ready?"

"Almost."

"Then shouldn't we…we…get the woman to bring our coats?"

Dana looked up from stacking gifts. "In just a minute, okay?"

He nodded. "Right."

She went back to her presents arranging and Aunt Nettie watched Les resume his incessant pacing. He paused at the windows now and then and watched the snow. Aunt Nettie spoke softly to Dana.

"He's rather like a child at times, isn't he?"

"Yes, except most children grow and learn, but a dementia victim never moves forward, only backward."

Aunt Nettie observed Les some more. He grew agitated and anxious as he paced. All of a sudden he charged over to his wife, startling not her, but her aging aunt.

"Did I wear my coat? Where's your coat? Shouldn't we be

getting out of here? It's snowing, Dana. Did you know it's snowing? You don't like driving in bad weather."

"Oh, my word," Aunt Nettie muttered.

Dana rose with a stack of gifts. She handed them to Les. "I think we can go now. Carry these for me, please."

He immediately took off around the room with the gifts, pacing again in circles as if he didn't know what else to do. Because he didn't. Aunt Nettie now looked dumbfounded. Dana took notice and tried to reassure the older woman.

"Les is out of his comfort zone here, Aunt Nettie. He gets this way sometimes when we leave our house now."

"However do you cope, my dear?"

"One day at a time, Aunt Nettie. One day at a time."

Her aunt drew Dana close for a hug, and then she followed Les out of the room. Abruptly, he swung around and came back. He embraced the old woman awkwardly around the presents.

"Merry Christmas, Aunt Nettie!"

* * *

On a cold January morning, Les sat behind the desk in his study playing a word game on the computer. Down on the lower level in the storage room, Dana sat on the floor and scrabbled through box after box, taking out items, looking them over, and putting them back. Everything from old household items to Gwen's and Graham's early school memorabilia. She mumbled as she worked.

"So, Miss Claire, O ye of the husband thieving, what did you give Les, foolish though it might have been, to keep you close to his heart? I guess I should've asked you that when we had our little tete-a-tete at your house before Christmas. When you were so free with your glasses of wine and your words of warning."

The phone jangled and Dana thought about answering on the old-fashioned wall phone over in the downstairs kitchen. But the ringing stopped before she could make up her mind. Seconds later, footsteps sounded overhead. They paused at the top of the steps. She had left the door open up there and Les called down to her.

"Dana, sweetheart, telephone."

"Who is it, Les?" she hollered.

"Your…your…you know…your Christmas aunt. Now what's her name?"

Dana grumbled her way to her feet, not bothering to reply, and stomped out of the storage area. She took the call in the kitchen on the old-time phone after all.

"Hi, Aunt Nettie."

The old lady traveled I-71 East from Beaumont Reserve swathed in furs in a chauffeur-driven limousine. In the rear seat she talked on the car phone, Booboo beside her, decked out in a fancy sweater. The pair of them looked as if they were off to the Ritz-Carlton for another holiday affair.

"What are you doing, my dear?"

"Oh…just sorting through some storage boxes."

"Whatever for?"

Dana released a frustrated sigh. "I'm looking for something."

"What? For goodness sake."

"I'm hoping I'll know when I find it."

"Well, stop that nonsense right now!" Aunt Nettie snapped. "And get yourself ready to go. I'll pick you up in half an hour. We'll do lunch, and then shop some of the sales at your mall."

At the Grand Oaks Indoor Plaza, Dana and Aunt Nettie, making her cumbersome way along with an elaborate walking stick, strolled down the main corridor among an array of shoppers. The chauffeur kept pace behind them, carrying tiny Booboo snuggled up on a small pillow in his arms, taking in everything and everyone.

"How can I help you with Les, my dear?" asked Aunt Nettie. "What do you need to care properly for him?"

Dana glanced over at the older woman. "Do you mean money? Thank you, but no, we don't need—"

"Never, my dear, *never* turn down monetary help. But that's not what I was referring to directly. A nurse, an aide, what help do you need that way? Even with insurance, the cost of his care will become enormous."

"Les still functions well at home right now. It's when he gets out of his comfort zone that he has trouble. As you saw at Christmas."

"How long before he can't function at all?"

Dana sighed wearily. She seemed to do a lot more of that lately.

"Dementia victims progress gradually, each at his or her own pace. The complete cycle typically takes years."

"A disease that turns intelligent human beings into pathetic imbeciles. Monstrous! I should leave my fortune to research."

"That would be wonderful, Aunt Nettie."

The old lady cackled. "I can hear the family now. They're all just waiting for me to die so they can inherit."

"You've said that before, but you know it's not true."

"Would serve them right if I didn't leave them a cent."

"Are you serious about leaving something to dementia research?"

"I don't know why not."

"The list of worthy causes for your money must be endless, Aunt Nettie, but as someone who lives with a dementia victim, I can tell you firsthand that, physical illness not withstanding—and I know some of them are beyond horrible—but even so, when you lose your short-term memory, you lose whatever quality of life you ever had. From there you can only live *in the moment.*"

* * *

Logs blazed in the fireplace in the hearth room at the Connelly's house. It was a blustery mid-morning in February. Les watched a courtroom drama on the big-screen TV from the comfort of his recliner. He had on an old pair of sweats. The phone rang and he reached for the handset on the side table. He checked the caller ID and answered.

"Hello, Claire."

"Hello, Les. What are you doing today?"

"Just watching TV."

"Let me guess," she said. "A courtroom drama. Which one?"

He stared at the TV screen, at the actors in a scene. "I don't remember the name of it. I'm sorry."

"Is Dana at home?"

"You called to talk to my wife?" Claire laughed while Les gave Dana's whereabouts some thought. "I think she's up in the shower."

"Is she going out?"

He looked thoughtful again. "I don't remember exactly. Something...maybe something with her...her friend Joan. What is it you...you women do?"

"Women's club?" When Les didn't respond, she asked, "Are they going out to lunch maybe? And shopping?"

"That sounds...I...I think that sounds right...Not a meeting. They're eating." He laughed like a child at his rhyming words.

"What do you think about a pair of former colleagues having lunch together?"

"Who? Oh, you mean us? You and me? Well, I don't...I don't...know."

"For old time's sake? What do you say?"

Les considered her suggestion. "I think...I think that would be...I suppose that would be okay."

"I'll see if I can get a reservation at the inn."

"What inn?"

"Our favorite seafood place. You remember. *Old Harbor Inn.* Across the river in Indiana."

"Oh, right. I think I do."

An hour later Dana backed her SUV out of the driveway and drove off. A few minutes later Claire's Lexus turned in from down the street and stopped in the drive. Les was pouring a mug of coffee in the kitchen when the doorbell chimed. He put down the carafe and went out to the foyer. When he opened the front door, Claire stood there smiling and holding a single long stem red rose. Red for love. She wore a striking pantsuit. He looked stunned to see her. He glanced around quickly. None of the neighbors was out and about just then. She handed the rose to him.

"Happy Valentine's Day!"

"Is it Valentine's Day? I forget these things now. I didn't get Dana anything."

"I came to take you to lunch, Les."

He looked around outside again. Were any of the neighbors watching?

"Claire, we...we...I don't...I don't think..."

"Have you forgotten my phone call this morning?"

"We talked this morning?"

"We agreed that former colleagues could do lunch," she

said. "What harm is there in that?"

"Well…"

They left Kentucky in Claire's Lexus via the John F. Kennedy Memorial Bridge over the Ohio River. They arrived at the *Old Harbor Inn* on Highway 56 on the Southern Indiana side of the river thirty minutes later. The rustic seafood restaurant overlooked the water. She parked in an empty spot in the lot out front among the lunch crowd. Inside the nautical-themed dining room, a long row of tall windows offered a cloudy-day view of the river winding through snowy woodlands. Logs burned low in a huge fireplace across the room.

They dined on seafood plates and beers. The rose Claire had given to Les lay next to his plate. He had settled in comfortably at the restaurant. It was familiar territory and brought back pleasant, long-term memories of meeting her here through the many years of their secret affair. But his peace didn't last. It couldn't. Not for a dementia victim out of his everyday orbit. The only orbit Les could reasonably inhabit.

Claire sensed his unease and tried to help. "This is our favorite seafood spot, Les. We've been coming here for seventeen years."

"Yes, I think I remember that."

But something bothered him in spite of the convivial atmosphere. He couldn't figure out what it was, though. Couldn't pin it down.

"Claire, I don't…I…I'm not…I'm not sure—"

He broke off when their server arrived with a smile. Pretty. Friendly. Casual.

"Can I get you guys anything else? Claire? Les? More beer?"

Les looked at Claire for help. But she didn't understand this simple need. Therefore, she left him, unwittingly, to flounder on his own. And flounder, he did.

"Uh…no…uh…I…no…uh…no, thank you…uh…Marcie."

"Sure, Les," the server replied, giving him a strange look, but she was good at handling the unexpected and went smoothly on. "I'll check back in just a bit. It's good to see you guys again. It's been a while."

Les watched Marcie move on to another table, and at last his brain grabbed hold of what bothered him. Where was Dana? Why wasn't she here with him? But she couldn't be, could she? Did she know he was here with Claire? Claire took his hand across the table and suddenly he forgot all about his wife. When he was with Claire, forgetting about Dana was easy. That's why he couldn't be with Claire anymore.

"We miss you at the office, Les." She squeezed his fingers. "Very much."

"I sure miss coming in," he replied. "Have you replaced me yet?"

She smiled, provocatively. "You're irreplaceable, my darling. Incomparable. Inimitable. Incandescent."

Les laughed. "And you're overdoing it. Just a bit." He lifted the rose next to his plate and laid it down again. "I don't have a Valentine gift for you. I'm sorry."

"You're the only gift I want." She squeezed his hand again. "I miss you *so* much, Les. Spending time with you whenever we could work it out."

"Haven't we talked about this?"

She didn't reply. Just watched him. Wary now. Afraid. Where was he going? Did he remember that they'd agreed not to see each other anymore? She'd counted on his memory loss working to her advantage there. As she'd told Dana, she had no intention of giving him up. She didn't lose, not in court and not in life.

"I think we've talked about this, Claire. I'm not much good

anymore. Mentally, I mean. I think I told you that we can't be together now. Didn't I?"

"Les, if I left the firm too, we could have all the time together that we couldn't have before. We could be retired together and do some traveling. When you get your divorce—"

"Dana and I are getting a divorce?"

"Well…yes…we talked about that possibility, and then you and I—"

Suddenly, Les gazed wildly around. "Where are we? I know this place, but I… I…forget. Where are we exactly? I get confused away from home now."

He stared across the table at the plea on her face. The plea that said—please don't do this. And he wanted to respond favorably, but he couldn't. He was too uncertain now, too unconnected, and most of all, too unwilling.

"Claire, I want to go home. I'm sorry."

* * *

Claire pulled her Lexus into the Connelly's driveway and stopped. Les got out with his rose. He closed the door and she backed up to the street and sped off as if she was late for a courtroom appearance before a cantankerous judge. At the front door he felt around in his pockets for his keys. At last, he pressed the bell. Dana opened the door in a minute, glanced around, and gawked at him.

"I must've forgotten my keys," he said.

"I was worried. I got home and there wasn't any note. Well, of course not. Not anymore. Where did you go, Les?"

He stepped past her into the foyer. "Don't ask me where I've been. It was just lunch, Dana."

She closed the door behind him, when he swung around

abruptly and came back. He handed her the long stem red rose.

"Happy Valentine's Day, sweetheart."

Les vanished into his office as if his life depended on it. And maybe it did at that moment. In the kitchen Dana stalked over to the counter and slid out the trash bin. She dropped the rose inside. "Nice try, Claire."

CHAPTER 11

On a warm, breezy May afternoon on the Connelly's back lawn, trees leafed out, fresh and green; flowers bloomed, arrayed with new color. A pair of blue jays fed a nest of babies on a lower limb in a spreading tree. Les finished mowing the grass, riding around the big yard on his shiny John Deere. He parked it by the garage as Dana came outside from the breakfast room onto the terrace. She carried a pitcher of lemonade and two tall glasses of ice on a tray and set them on the table. He shut off the mower and joined her. And she was reminded of the scene earlier in the garage with the lawn mower. He couldn't remember how to start it and called for her help. She was surprised by that at first. Why didn't he ask their neighbor and friend next door? Then she realized why. He didn't want the man to know that he couldn't remember how to start his own lawn mower. So she assessed the unfamiliar situation and decided that after filling the gas tank from a refill can by the workbench, he needed to open the choke, put the thing in gear, insert the key into the ignition and turn it. Could the problem be solved any easier? Well, maybe the oil should be changed, she reasoned, if lawn mowers were anything like cars. But that could probably wait. She released a grateful sigh, and then came the big question: where was the key? Following a frantic search in which Les nearly caused both of them to blow a gasket—pun fully intended—he at last located it among the debris on his workbench.

They sat down at the table on the terrace and she poured their lemonades. He drank most of his in one long gulp. She sipped hers.

"The…the birds," he began, "oh, what are they? The…the blues…the blue jays! They've got four babies."

She didn't comment and he refilled his glass and drank. The next door neighbor rode past on his lawn mower. He waved and Les waved back.

"I'm glad I cancelled our lawn service," he told Dana, encompassing the lawn with a sweep of his hand. "Burke next door cancelled his service too. He said he's another do-it-yourselfer since he retired. I love doing all this myself."

A few minutes went by. He watched nature's various activities around the yard, and she watched him while she drank some more of her lemonade.

Les said, "Did I tell you? The blues…the blue jays…they've got four babies in the nest. Those little guys sure do keep mama and daddy busy feeding them. Nature's amazing, isn't it? How they instinctively care for their own?"

Dana still didn't say anything, but now she stood and went back inside. She returned with Claire's anniversary card in the envelope and sat down again. She laid the envelope on the table in front of him. He glanced at it.

"What's this?"

When she didn't answer, he picked up the envelope and squinted at his name handwritten on the front. He removed the anniversary card and reached into his front shirt pocket for his reading glasses. He came up empty.

"I don't have my glasses."

She went back inside and brought them out to him. She returned to her seat and handed his glasses across the table. He slipped them on and read the front of the card—HAPPY ANNIVERSARY TO THE ONE I LOVE.

"Did I forget our anniversary, sweetheart?"

He opened the card, read the inside verse, the signature and the note. When he finished, he sat there, thunderstruck. For the longest time he couldn't look at her. Then slowly, his gaze lifted and met Dana's. He didn't want to face this. Didn't want to face her. But he couldn't look away now. Where did she get this card? He didn't even remember it. Curse his memory loss! Curse this whole dementia mess that had happened to him! Except dementia didn't affect long-term memory loss. He'd simply forgotten about the card over all this time. He slipped off his readers and dropped them on the table. He stared at his wife. She stared back. Seconds ticked by like the sound of an eternity passing between them.

"Where is it, Les?"

"What?"

"You heard what I said."

"Yes, I heard you, but what are you talking about? Where is what?"

She recited the note written in the card from memory: "I hope the gift that I gave you seventeen years ago, foolish though it might have been, still keeps us close to your heart when we're not together."

He looked as lost as he was. "I have no idea."

She examined him carefully. "No, I guess you don't."

"Where did you get this card?"

"I came across it when I helped you pack up your office. The day after your retirement party. It fell out of an old law book.

Les, will you talk to me about this?"

He thought that over for a minute. "What do you expect me to say?"

"I expect you to say what's in your heart."

"What's in my heart is this: I'm sorry."

They stared at each other. Time came to a stop. The birds didn't chirp. The breeze didn't blow. The sun didn't shine. That was how it seemed to them.

Finally, Dana broke the awful silence between them. "That's it? You're sorry. That's all you have to say?"

"I…I don't…I…What do you…you mean? What else do you want?"

"Can you give me some clarity here? Are you sorry that you had the affair? Or are you just sorry that I found out?"

He stared at his wife some more, at a loss for words now.

"Why did you and Claire have an affair for most of our married life?"

"I don't…I don't know…how…how to…I…I can't explain."

"Have I been a fool all these years? I thought we were so much in love. I thought we were happy."

"I thought so too."

"Do you love Claire?"

Les glanced away, at their neighbor riding his mower over the grass. At last, his eyes came back to Dana and she saw all of his pain in that one look.

"It *is* possible for a man to love two women. I know in…in our culture that's more or less frowned upon. Even…even forbidden. But is…is it really so difficult to…to believe?"

"So it wasn't ever just a sexual relationship?"

"No."

"Then why are you still with me?"

"Because I love you, sweetheart. And I…I'm sorry. I…I'm so

sorry. I didn't ever want you and the kids to be hurt. Believe me, I…I didn't."

"You just wanted to have one life with us and a second life separate from us?"

"I know that's how it must seem to you. But whatever it was, I…well, I did it. I did it, Dana…I don't know why…exactly…Claire just…we…we…she loves me…and I…I…I'm sorry. I believe in the sanctity of marriage, but…"

"But what?"

"I don't know! I just don't know how I can explain! And I'm so sorry!"

"So what do you want now?"

He looked at her for the longest time. Didn't she know?

"I want my memory back. I want to be a lawyer again. And most of all, I don't want to lose you and the kids."

"What about Claire?"

"I think…I…I think I gave her up. And I'd give anything if you hadn't found out about her. Because I've…I've hurt you and I'd rather die than hurt you, sweetheart."

* * *

Les sat on the bed up in the master suite a few evenings later dressed only in his boxers and a T-shirt. He wore his glasses and talked on the phone. He held a pen and scribbled in a notepad on his lap.

"Yes, that's correct. The directions to your restaurant, please. Your—what? Do I have a GPS?...GPS?...in my car?...Oh, that! Yes! But I…I won't be the one driving…No, I…the driver…she…that is…she…No, this is a surprise. Could you just give me the directions to your restaurant, please? No, your automated message goes too quickly for me and I can't get the directions written down…No, I…I don't use the Internet so much…Yes, I…I appreciate your help, thank you. We'll be coming from across the river on I-71 East in Kentucky."

He listened and wrote on the pad. In the adjoining bathroom, Dana took a shower, oblivious to what her husband was doing. Had she known, she'd have happily throttled him. And had Les understood what crime he was about to commit, he would've jumped off the planet rather than do it.

A short time later, Les came out of his walk-in closet wearing dress pants and a button-down shirt. He entered Dana's closet in time to zip up the back of her long, summer dress. He kissed her neck.

"Let's dance."

She eased away from him. "Why won't you tell me where we're going?"

"Because it's a surprise."

She noted his clothes, minus a suit jacket. "Where's your blazer?"

"Too hot for a blazer."

She faced him, her mouth open for a retort. But he turned suddenly and walked out. He wasn't about to discuss his attire. She made an ugly face at his back. And then she laughed at herself. She might as well laugh as cry about these kinds of things. There was little enough humor in the downhill life of a dementia victim.

* * *

The Kentucky Center was located on Main Street in downtown Louisville. Three hours later Dana and Les descended the theater's sweeping steps amid the semi-formal crowd. He held onto her arm as they maneuvered their way down.

"You're amazing, Les," she said. "You remembered how much I've been wanting to see this touring Broadway play."

"I heard you telling Joan about it on the phone one day and I wrote down the name of the play and where it would be showing. So I wouldn't forget to order the tickets. Pete picked them up for me. I clipped them to my new crossword book, so I wouldn't forget I had them."

"So we owe Pete for the tickets?"

"No. I gave him my credit card info to use."

They reached the bottom step and aimed toward the parking garage down the street where they'd left her SUV. Ten minutes later they crossed the John F. Kennedy Memorial Bridge into Southern Indiana. According to his handwritten directions, they followed I-65 north to Highway 56 and arrived at the *Old Harbor Inn* on the Ohio River a half an hour later.

In the foyer Les approached the hostess who was dressed in a long gown, while Dana headed toward the restrooms sign. The hostess was tall, slender and attractive.

"Good evening," he said. "We have a reservation. Les and Dana Connelly."

"Of course, Mr. Connelly. Let me check on that."

Dana rejoined Les in a minute as the hostess returned from her station.

"Come this way, please," she said.

They followed the woman to a window table with a spanning view of moonlight glistening off the river. She left them with embossed menus, promising that a server would be along right away. Dana gazed around the nautical-themed dining room. Les reached for her hand across the table.

He said, "Have I told you how gorgeous you look tonight?"

She smiled. "So now tell me about this restaurant."

He smiled. "It's your favorite seafood place, sweetheart."

She stared at him. A sudden chill went down her back, and it wasn't caused by the sudden fresh burst from the air conditioning. "I've never been here before, Les."

Marcie, the server who always took care of Les and Claire on their former regular visits, arrived at their table, coming up behind Dana.

"I almost didn't recognize you," she said. "You've changed your hair." She stepped around Dana's chair. "I really like the new color, Clai—"

Marcie slammed to an embarrassing halt, realizing her mistake. Hardly anyone as young as she was blushed these days, but this innocent lamb sure did. She became red as a radish in the time it took her to look from Dana to Les. But give the young woman credit, she recovered well.

"May I take your drink order, Les?"

Before he could say a word in reply, Dana eased her chair back and stood. "Excuse me, please. I won't be long."

She did a blind rush through the dining room, weaving among the tables of diners, trying to hold her expression in place and keep her mind on auto pilot. If she let even one thought creep in, she would lose her cool like a snowball way down there in you-know-where before she arrived at her destination. Again.

Alone at the vanity in the lounge, she stared at her reflection in the mirror. She watched her eyes glaze over. No! She wasn't going to cry! She wasn't! That's not how she handled adversity. She'd gone through a crying period over this Claire thing, yes, but she'd been through a tremendous shock in learning of Les's infidelity. Now she'd succeeded in regaining control and wasn't about to lose it again. Okay. That settled, Dana returned to the dining room. She passed two chattering magpies as she entered.

Les glanced up from his menu when Dana walked up to

their table a few minutes later. She'd only been gone long enough to build up a fine anger. At Les. At Claire. At herself. She just couldn't figure out why she should be angry with herself. Two mugs of beer sat on the table. One in front of Les. One in front of her seat. She stared at them.

"I ordered your favorite beer," he said, going back to his menu.

"You know I don't drink beer, Les. I don't even like the smell."

He looked up. "What did you say, sweetheart?"

She heaved a ragged breath. She couldn't do this. She wouldn't do it. "Les, could we just go?"

Twenty minutes later Dana's SUV traveled south on I-65 in Southern Indiana, moving along in light traffic. They night sky grew dusky and stars twinkled into view.

Back on the Kentucky side of the river, she connected with I-71 East, heading toward Grand Oaks Village. Les gazed out at the darkness falling over the landscape like an encompassing blanket.

"We haven't eaten dinner, have we?" he asked. "You want to stop and get something? I know you don't go for fast food, but I sure could eat a quick burger."

When she didn't respond, he glanced over at her in the dim light from the dashboard. Her profile looked strange. Was she angry with him?

CHAPTER 12

Pots and pans littered the kitchen counters at the Connelly's house. Dishes crowded the sink. Drawers and cabinet doors hung open. The following day, about mid-morning, Les poured pancake batter onto the griddle at the cook-top in the center island. Dana wandered in, barely conscious and yawning into her hands. She stopped short on her way to the coffeemaker, taking in the kitchen. She stared at the chaos and suddenly she was wide awake and functioning.

Les glanced up at her and smiled. "Morning, sweetheart. I'll have breakfast ready here before you know it."

Her mood hadn't improved any from the night before so she ignored him and made her way around the room, slamming doors and banging drawers as she went. She reached for a mug in a cabinet above her head.

"Les, when you cook, do you have to use every container and utensil we own? Tilly's not here today. So this mess is all yours. *I'm* not cleaning it up."

She poured coffee and sniffed the enticing aroma. It was fuel for her angry fire so she added insult to injury.

"Don't make any pancakes for me. A three-minute egg and toast sounds like a good idea to me."

Happily flipping pancakes, Les deflated like a punctured

balloon. He dropped a pancake on the floor, and when he bent to retrieve it he knocked over the bowl of batter. It spilled and ran all over the counter, down the lower cabinet doors and onto the floor. She rolled her eyes and took a sip of coffee as she strolled out. Served him right.

The next afternoon in the laundry room upstairs in the bedroom wing, Dana, still in grumpy mode, yanked open drawers and pounded them shut. Finally, she stepped out into the hallway and called down the stairs.

"Les, will you come up here?"

She didn't add a considerate "please" to her request because considerate was the last word anyone would use to describe her these days. But Les—if you liked the word *irony*—was blessed with little, if any, memory of yesterday and his wife's dismal mood. And so he hurried up to her with childlike innocence. She whammed another drawer closed as he strode into the laundry room, all smiles and anticipation.

"Did you call me, sweetheart?"

"What did you do with that hard-plastic hammer? You know the one I like so much. I keep it right here in this drawer." She indicated the one she meant. "I saw you with it earlier today."

"What was I doing?"

"I don't know! I was on the computer. I just saw you go by with it."

"I...I don't remember...I'm sorry."

She rejected his apology and lashed out. "Can't you remember anything?" She slammed another cabinet door and stormed off. "Why can't you ever put things back when you finish with them?"

He watched her huff out of the room and down the steps, looking completely dejected and lost. She'd be so much better off if he didn't live here anymore.

In the master suite late the following morning, Dana was still on her rampage. She put away Les's clean socks and briefs that he'd left lying on the chest of drawers when he'd dressed earlier. As she sorted through a confusion of items already inside the drawers, he strolled in and she pounced on him. A cat going after a canary.

"Your drawers are a mess! What? A tornado touched down in here and decided to stay? Why must you always turn nice and neat into topsy-turvy?"

"I do that?" he asked, bewildered.

She sighed with frustration, threw up her hands and stalked out. "Why don't you finish this job? See if you can do something right for a change!"

* * *

Rain fell steadily the following afternoon en route to an appointment with his neurologist, Dr. Heyburn, in Lakewood. Dana's SUV followed slowly behind an old silver Jaguar XKE convertible (top up) in mint condition, while Les gazed idly out the windshield at it. She tapped her horn when the tardy driver began to wear on her nerves.

"Come on already! Christmas will be here before you get where you're going!"

Les said, "He or she, I can't tell through the rain, is probably obeying the speed limit. Which is a good idea in this weather."

"What?" She all but screamed. "Now you're telling me how to drive!"

He glanced over at her and shifted into injured mode, staring out the passenger's window. Pleasing his wife these days seemed to be an impossibility, and he only wished that he could figure out what to do about it.

* * *

Dr. Heyburn gave Les a C, using his old high school report card language regarding his mental condition. Which, translated, meant that he was an average patient, doing better than some, but not as well as others in his progression along dementia's downward spiral. On the drive back from the doctor visit, Dana had had enough of mental illness and all of its resident trappings for a while. She needed a break and stopped at the Grand Oaks Indoor Plaza. With blatant disregard for her husband, she told him that he could either tag along on what surely would be a lengthy and boring trip for him, or wait almost forever in the car until she returned. But she'd leave him the keys to access the air and the CD player, she added. After all, she wasn't completely heartless.

He wanted her to take him home and come back to do her shopping. She wanted him to stop hallucinating and try facing reality for a change. In the end he trailed his belligerent wife around the shops, lugging her purchases and keeping his mouth shut.

* * *

Dana relaxed at the table on the terrace behind their house the next afternoon with a glass of iced tea. She watched the blue jay family. At the nest the mama and daddy fed their hungry brood. Les came outside from the breakfast room and walked over. She glanced up at him like he was something messy that she'd just stepped in.

He said, "I think I've broken your heart and I don't know

how to fix it."

* * *

Dana and Joan went on a power walk in shorts and tees along a meandering path in Grand Oaks Park a few days later. Birds trilled among the tree branches. Squirrels and chipmunks scampered around in the grass.

"I showed Claire's card to Les," Dana said. "And he admitted everything."

"But he'll forget telling you, won't he? He probably already has."

"No, he won't forget *that* conversation. Because it involved emotion. His neuro doc told us early on how emotional memory is different from other memory. That it travels a different path in the brain."

"Interesting," Joan said as they crossed a gurgling creek over an arced bridge.

"I think Les is truly sorry for his affair," Dana went on. "Because he wound up hurting me. And I needed to hear that, but…"

"But sorry is just not enough."

"Joan, I think I hate him. He tried to make amends…"

"How do you make up for a seventeen-year affair? Some things can't be corrected, my sweet."

"He took me to a touring Broadway play at the Kentucky Center in Louisville. The play I told you about. He overheard me telling you and ordered the tickets. Then we went out to dinner at Claire's favorite restaurant. Les got mixed up. He thought it was *my* favorite."

"Oh, sweetie."

"He ordered a beer for me—Claire probably likes beer—but

he forgot that I don't drink it. You know that I don't even like the smell."

They paused along the walkway and Joan tried not to laugh, but she couldn't help herself. Suddenly, she was laughing and couldn't stop.

"I'm sorry, Dana…I know it's not funny, but…I just…"

Joan's hysterical laugh was contagious and Dana couldn't help joining in. They laughed and laughed so hard that they had to sit down on a nearby bench to catch their breath. They finally stopped laughing, but when they looked at each other they started up again. And this next session went on for a good, healing five minutes.

* * *

Dana's SUV swung into the driveway and the garage door rolled up. Following her jaunt in the park with Joan, they topped off the day with lunch at *The Garden Gate* restaurant that included an entire bottle of their best wine. She was in a much better mindset after the restoring time with her best friend. She'd even decided to apologize to her husband for treating him so shabbily in recent days. And it wasn't just the wine talking. She was sincere and ashamed. She knew that Les wasn't to blame for his mental condition. How could she have been so cruel to him? But she knew also that he'd forgive her. Forgiveness had always been one of his choicest qualities. Remarkable for a lawyer, but there it was. She'd realized a long time ago that, contrary to accepted opinion, it wasn't the lawyer who made the man, but the man who made the lawyer.

Dana entered the house via the short hallway leading from the garage. Anxious now to make amends, she called Les's name but didn't get a response. She checked and he wasn't in the kitchen, breakfast bay, or hearth room. Through the windows, she took in the empty back lawn and terrace. She opened the door leading down to the lower level, shouted for him, and got nothing. She breezed past his vacant study and gave the living room and dining room a cursory glance. He wasn't in either of those rooms. She even peeked into the half bath before climbing the front staircase. On the second floor, Dana went into the master bedroom and bath and came right back out. She gave Gwen's and Graham's bedrooms and baths a quick check as well as the guest room and bath, plus the laundry area. Les wasn't anywhere in the house. What should she do now?

Two hours later she still roamed their neighborhood on foot, hunting for her errant husband and chatting up the neighbors. Had anyone seen him today? Had anyone even talked to him? She took out her cell phone one more time as she headed back home. She'd called all of their family and friends and no one had had a clue to his whereabouts.

But she hadn't been able to reach Graham. She'd left a message, but maybe he hadn't checked it yet. She'd give him another try.

* * *

At the same time, Graham drove his black BMW randomly around Louisville. Les sat in the passenger's seat observing the scenery flashing by as if he'd never seen any of it before. For him this was true because he couldn't remember how most of it looked.

"Dad, we've been driving around for hours," Graham said. "Have you decided where you want to go?"

"I don't know."

"What's going on? I know I keep asking you this, but…What's with your luggage? Why did you bring it?"

Les looked at his son. "My luggage?"

"I think you're confused today, Dad. Why wouldn't you let me take Mom's call a while ago?"

Exactly on cue Graham's cell phone came to life on the console between them.

They both reached for it. Les got there first and grabbed it. He squinted at the caller ID.

"I think it's your mom. I can't be sure without my glasses."

Graham's hand shot out for the phone. "Let me talk to her. This is the second time she's called."

Les jerked away with the cell, holding it out of Graham's reach while it rang and rang. "No! No mom! No more mom!"

"Dad, please."

"I'm not…I think…I'm…I think…I can't bother your mom."

"*What*?"

Graham's cell stopped chirping and his voicemail message kicked in. Dana's voice came on next, asking her son to please call her as soon as he could. This was twice that she'd left a message saying it was urgent that she speak to him regarding his dad.

Les said, "There's no mom. There's no more mom."

Graham stopped at a traffic light and stared at his father. "Dad, you…listen to me, you're just a little confused right now. But it's okay. Just let me talk to mom and we can straighten this all out."

Graham tried to gently take back his cell phone, but Les drew up against the passenger's window as a resistant child might and wouldn't let go of it. The light flashed green and his son heaved a grave sigh and drove on.

"Where's *your* cell phone, Dad?"

"I don't...I think...I...I'm ...I don't know."

"Okay. So about your luggage. Are you and mom going on a trip?"

"I don't think so."

"How about I take you back home now?"

"I don't...I don't think I can go back there."

Graham shot his dad a quick look. "Why not?"

There was no reply from Les. He just hugged the window clutching Graham's cell phone as if it was his greatest treasure.

"We should call mom. She's worried about you. That's why she keeps calling."

"She's not worried."

Another heavy sigh from Graham. "Can you help me out here a little, Dad? Did you and mom have an argument? Do you remember an argument?"

"I don't think so. Your mom and I don't argue, son. You know that."

"Well, something's wrong."

* * *

Twenty minutes later in the kitchen at the Connelly's house, Dana heated a mug of coffee in the microwave. The buzzer dinged and she popped the door open and removed her mug. She blew and sipped and paced around. The phone on the computer desk jingled in the breakfast room. She put down her coffee on the center island and almost ran for it. She answered without even checking the caller ID.

"Hello."

Graham said, "Mom, I've never seen Dad so mixed up. He's totally clueless today. What's going on with his luggage?"

"Oh, my. I didn't even think to check that. He's got his

luggage?"

"I drove him around all afternoon, but he couldn't tell me what he wanted to do. I don't think he knew. And I...I mean this is going to sound crazy, but I think he's scared to come home. What's happening, Mom?"

"Scared to come home? Oh, honey, your father's well...oh...he's troubled."

Graham laughed. 'You think so?"

"It's all my fault. I haven't been very...well...I haven't been very understanding lately. To put it mildly. And I am sorry. Graham, where's your dad now?"

CHAPTER 13

On the fourth floor of the Oaks office building on Brownsboro Road, Claire sat behind the desk in her office at the law firm focused on the brief she was writing out on a yellow legal pad. Stacks of briefs, motions and trial preparations filled her desk. Suddenly, she lifted her eyes. Les stood in the open doorway, a piece of luggage in each hand. She beamed at him and jumped up, dropping her pen on the long pad. She went past him and pushed the office door closed. He set down his suitcases and she embraced him from behind. Then she stepped around and gave him a full-blown hug. He hugged her back and they kissed. She made it long and deep and passionate.

At last, he drew away. "You don't know how good this feels," he said, "to hold and kiss someone who wants me."

"I knew you'd come. I knew you would." She kissed him until they both ran out of breath. "We've only just begun, Les. Again. So tell me what happened?"

"What happened?"

"With Dana. Why did you leave?"

"I can't...I don't...exactly...I don't want to talk about her."

"That's the best news I've ever heard." She led him over to the leather sofa. "Come and sit down, and we'll talk about us."

* * *

In the kitchen at the Connelly's house, Dana paced about some more with her coffee mug. In the foyer the front door opened and footsteps hit the floor running.

"Mom!" Gwen shouted, heading for the back of the house. "Graham just called."

In the breakfast room, Gwen met her mom coming toward her. "He said he couldn't tell you on the phone. He just couldn't. I told him I was coming over anyway. So he didn't have to. I think he's glad he doesn't have to face you with this."

Alarmed now, Dana said, "Has something happened to your dad?"

Minutes later, mother and daughter sat at the table on the terrace, both of them with coffee mugs. A soft breeze surrounded them. Birds twittered in the trees.

"If Graham left Dad at the office," Gwen said, "that means Claire Breen."

Dana nodded her agreement and stared into her coffee.

"Are you okay with that?"

"Do I have a choice?"

Gwen sighed heavily. "I told Graham about Dad and Claire. He has a right to know, Mom. Why didn't you tell him?"

Dana stared at Gwen and chewed on her bottom lip.

* * *

An hour later Dana's SUV turned into the parking lot at River Road Landing. She found a vacant space and parked among the other vehicles. She didn't see her son's car, but got out anyway and walked along the wharf to the houseboat that he shared with two of his friends. The old life preserver, the rusted anchor, and the dirty fishnet decorating the boat reminded her of that seafood restaurant where Les had taken her. She paused and glanced around.

"Graham?...Anybody home?...Graham?...Juno?...Dallas?..."

No response. So she stepped aboard, grabbing the rail quickly as the boat rocked beneath her. She took a seat in a deck chair. A T-shirt draped another chair. A pair of flip flops and a copy of *The Courier Journal* lay haphazardly around a third chair. She relaxed and waited, watching as other boats departed and returned to their respective slips. Cabin cruisers. Sailboats. Fishing rigs. Runabouts. Time passed and she checked her watch. She waited some more. At last, Graham ambled down the wharf from the direction of the parking lot. He boarded the houseboat and just stood there for a minute, hands on his hips, grinning at his mother. She smiled and tried to look innocent. She failed and he laughed, not at her but with her. She hadn't been fair to him regarding the situation with Les. And they both knew it.

"I came to buy you dinner, honey."

Graham laughed again. "No, you came to buy *me*."

Dana suddenly looked as guilty as she felt.

"That's better," her son said. "You want something to drink?"

"Yes, please."

He disappeared inside the boat and came back with a can of beer and a can of soda. He gave the soda to his mom and flopped on the chair next to her. He snapped the top on the beer and swallowed an ample drink. She opened her drink and sipped. They observed as a van turned into the lot and parked. A middle-aged man and woman got out, unloaded several bags, and started walking toward them.

Graham said, "You should've told me."

"I know. And I apologize. I shouldn't have confided in Gwen, but since I did you were entitled to the same. I am sorry."

"So, only telling Gwenie. That was some chick thing with you two?"

Dana heaved a long sigh of resignation. The middle-aged couple strolled past them carrying grocery bags. The man nodded and Graham slugged more of his beer and saluted the man with the can.

"I guess. Something like that, anyway." She took another sip of her soda. "Are you shocked at your dad?"

"Totally blown away. I mean, some men…yeah…sure…you know…but Dad? Come on. No way."

"It *was* a shock."

"So will you guys get a divorce now?"

"If that's what your dad wants."

"Mom, he doesn't know what he wants. He's sick."

"I think he's made up his mind. He went to Claire."

"Maybe she'll bring him back after a week of explaining the same thing to him ten times in an hour." He shook his head.

"When I took Dad fishing…he was…I mean, he tried, but…he made me crazy. I didn't let on, but I sure don't know how you do it day in and day out. Claire Breen has no idea what she's in for."

"Until you live with a dementia victim, you can't understand. It's all just words. But she can keep him. And when he can't remember which drawer his socks are in, the same drawer they've been in for the last fifteen years, she can just deal with it."

Graham studied his mom. "You mean that?"

"Your dad left *me*. He doesn't want me anymore."

"Maybe Dad left because he thinks you don't want *him* anymore."

She stared at her son in awe, as if she hadn't thought of the situation that way.

* * *

That night in the fitness room on the lower level of the house, Dana's footfalls pounded the treadmill. She worked out as if all the devil's demons were chasing her at the same time, pushing herself beyond the limit. Pushing. Pushing. Trying to push everything away. Les. His dementia. Claire. Their affair. Classical music played on the sound system, but she only heard Graham's words at the boat: *maybe Dad left because he thinks you don't want* him *anymore.*

The phone jangled in the breakfast room the next morning as Dana padded in wearing her nightgown and looking sleepy. She picked up the handset on the computer desk, checking the caller ID first.

"Morning, Gwen."

"What are you doing, Mom?"

She streaked toward the empty coffeemaker on the kitchen counter, suddenly reminded of how Les always had the coffee going for her in the mornings.

"Oh, I...I'm thinking about coffee."

"What about the rest of the day?"

At the sink she rinsed and filled the carafe with fresh cold water. "I think I need to look for a job. When your dad and I get down to the basics of the divorce—"

"Whoa! Where did that come from? Before you said..."

"Of course he'll want a divorce. Everything's in both of our names, but I want to...I need to...work. Keep busy, I mean. Oh,

I know I've been out of the workforce for a long time, but—"

"Wait a minute, Mom—"

"Why wait? I need a new focus, honey. Maybe I can find *something*, some kind of job. And part-time would be nice. Then I'd still have time for some volunteer work. I've got to dig up my old résumé."

"Sounds as though you're getting on with your life."

Dana opened a cabinet door above the coffeemaker and took out a can of grounds. "Sure I am. Getting on with my life. And it…oh…it'll be tough…different…but…"

"You can do it. Oh, you know what? I've been doing a lot of thinking and I've come up with a great idea! How would you like to get away for a few days? Now that my classes are over for the summer, why don't we go somewhere? Wouldn't that be fun? Just you and me. A mother-daughter trip."

* * *

The Belle of Louisville was an historic paddlewheeler steamboat with two decks of old-world charm and Victorian décor. Dana and Gwen joined fellow passengers of all ages for three days and two nights on a delightful riverboat cruise down the Ohio and Mississippi Rivers. They journeyed through amazing forests and swamps, and passed by tumbling rapids and huge dams, and stopped at charming small towns. They fished from the lower deck in the mornings assisted by a helpful instructor. Followed by a sumptuous brunch buffet complete with a professional storyteller in period attire that included a bowtie and high-button shoes. With his own flair for style, the man taught them about related sections of American history.

"…and the Belle of Louisville is the oldest steamboat still operating in the United States. This grand old lady's been churning these waters for more than ninety years..."

In the afternoons Dana and Gwen had lazy conversations from loungers on the upper deck, getting acquainted with their traveling companions. During scheduled stops, they all strolled along the shore, shaded by great drooping tree branches and serenaded by melodic birdsong.

At evening cocktails, Dana and Gwen mixed and mingled. Seated at a long table for a formal candlelight dinner, they chatted with new acquaintances while a seven-piece orchestra played everything from the Beatles to Beethoven with Elvis in the middle. During the after-dinner dancing—a mixture of leisurely and lively—Gwen was beset with partners and settled in with a studious-looking hunk of eye-candy. Wyatt Carpenter's new wire-frame glasses made him look sexier than ever. And he had eyes only for Gwen from the moment they met. It was her smile, Wyatt said later. She'd just knocked his socks off. But he wasn't wearing socks, Gwen pointed out. And that was because she'd knocked him senseless, he countered with amusement.

Several middle-aged men sought out Dana for dancing and she managed to be polite enough to all of them, but clearly she wasn't interested in any particular one. So while Gwen strolled along the decks with wonderful Wyatt, sipping cold drinks and watching the sunset sparkle on the water, her mom relaxed with a boring book in their stateroom. Late on the last night out, Gwen packed her clothes while Dana arranged her cosmetic bag and other items into her luggage.

"I'm so ready to go home," Dana said.

Gwen glanced up from her packing. "You didn't have a good time, did you?"

"I had a very nice time, honey, but I'm sure some people think we only came on this trip to troll for men."

Her daughter sank down on the bed and subsided into laughter. In a minute she said, "Do we really care what anybody thinks?"

Dana smiled. "Well, no, I guess not."

"Wyatt and I...Oh, Mom, what do you think of him?"

"I like him. A lot. Tell me more about him."

"He's doing his residency at Jewish Hospital. Not kids, though. Geriatrics."

"So, two doctors in the family," Dana teased.

"Mom! You shouldn't be counting your baby chicks before you've even got a rooster crowing in your barnyard."

Dana stared at her. "Now where did *that* come from?"

"Wyatt's gram. He told me that's her favorite old maxim. She was raised in the country, in case you hadn't guessed."

"Well, from what I saw of you two," Dana said with a big smile, "I think we've definitely got a rooster crowing in *our* barnyard."

Gwen broke into laughter again.

The Belle of Louisville docked at River Road Landing early the next morning. Dana, Gwen and Wyatt were wedged among the passengers hugging the rails on the double decks and looking refreshed. Graham and Leah waited on the pier to greet them.

* * *

In the garage the next afternoon, Dana rummaged around Les's workbench, searching for anything that didn't seem to belong. She foraged in the bins and drawers and hunted among the clutter that had accumulated on the floor.

"What did you give to him, Claire?" she mumbled, "Foolish though it might have been. *What*?"

Finally, two hours later, she flopped down on in old lawn chair by the workbench with a grumbling sigh. She was completely done in. "I give up!"

That night she soaked in a bubble bath in the whirlpool tub in the master bathroom surrounded by flaming pillar candles. She sipped white wine from a slender glass and looked desolate. All of a sudden she recalled Graham's words again: *maybe Dad left because he thinks you don't want* him *anymore*

The wine helped Dana get to sleep later, but even so she tossed and turned and woke up more than once. She gazed over longingly at the vacant half of the bed. She sniffed Les's pillow and drew in his dear scent that she loved so well. A few days ago she didn't care that he had left. She'd even wanted him to go, but now that he was gone…oh, how she missed him! It seemed that she had developed an ache that wouldn't go away. What on earth had she done?

Dana sat at the table on the terrace the following morning with a mug of coffee. She watched the blue jay family in the nearby tree while mama and daddy taught their young how to fly. She smiled and remembered.

* * *

It was a summer evening twelve years ago when Gwen and Graham were ten years old. They hurried from the house wearing their backpacks and crossing the back lawn to the treehouse built into the huge old sycamore at the rear of the property. Dana and Les trailed the kids at a distance, lugging a heavy cooler between them.

Les said, "There's enough stuff in here to last them a week, not just overnight."

"They'll stay up all night seeing how much they can eat,"

Dana replied.

Gwen plunged into a run, calling over her shoulder to her brother. "I'll beat you up in the treehouse!"

Graham raced after her. "No way!"

Gwen kept the lead in spite of his effort to catch up. "I got born before you did, remember. You took so long getting here that the doctor thought you weren't ever coming out of mama."

Graham suddenly passed his sister in a herculean burst of speed. "So?"

Gwen sprinted ahead again. "So I can do anything faster than you can!"

Dana and Les laughed and watched Gwen climb the ladder to the treehouse first. Graham scrambled up after her as their parents reached the tree and gratefully sat down the cumbersome cooler. A few minutes later they strolled up on the terrace.

Dana said, "This is their first sleepover in the treehouse."

Les slipped an arm around his wife. "Sweetheart, they'll be fine."

"I don't know."

She turned and looked back at the kids up in the tree arranging the contents of their backpacks. Blankets. Pillows. Radio. Flashlights.

"Bet I can take your mind off the kids," he said.

They hugged and kissed, and gradually affection changed to passion and they went inside. Where he indeed succeeded in taking her mind off the kids.

* * *

Dana blinked hard and mentally shoved her memories away. Too bitter. Too sweet. She took a drink of cooled coffee and set the mug down. Beneath the nearby tree, a blue jay baby fluttered its wings. She smiled.

That afternoon Dana carried up the old family photo album from the storage room downstairs. She sat on the sofa in the hearth room and resumed her solitary trek down Memory Lane. She couldn't help it. Missing Les just wouldn't go away. If she couldn't be with him, at least she could look at treasured pictures of him. And if that wasn't enough, she'd drag out their old videos. If she could find the camera. On second thought, that might be too much for her to handle. So she contented herself with going through the album, turning pages, pausing, smiling. She stared at a picture and laughed all of a sudden. Then she laughed some more.

"I'd forgotten all about that!"

The front door opened and footsteps sounded in the foyer.

"Mom! You home?" Gwen called.

"Back here, honey!'

Minutes later Dana and Gwen huddled together, reminiscing through the family album, chatting like magpies and laughing like hyenas.

"Oh, that's our first Christmas!" Gwen said. "Look at Graham and me! We never did look like twins, did we? I'm glad you didn't dress us alike all the time."

"Your dad and I always considered you each distinctly different little people. Because that's who you were."

Gwen flipped a page and pointed to a picture. "First grade Christmas pageant. Mom, remember how silly I acted because Graham got to be Joseph, but I didn't get to play Mary? I just wanted to hold baby Jesus so much."

Dana turned a page and said, "Oh, here's your thirteenth birthday party. Teenagers at last."

"And there's Graham, hogging all the birthday cake. As

usual."

The front door opened again and heavier footfalls sounded in the foyer this time. Then the birthday-cake hog called out, "Where is everybody?"

Gwen put a finger to her lips. She whispered, "Don't answer, Mom."

Dana looked over at her daughter and they giggled together like little girls with a big secret. Graham found them that way a minute later and laughed too as he dropped down on the sofa beside his mom.

"You guys think you're hiding back here or something?"

Gwen pointed out the thirteenth birthday party picture in which Graham was helping himself to what was left of the cake.

"Look at yourself, showoff."

"I remember that cake!" Graham said. "That's the best one we ever had, Mom."

As the three of them continued through the album together, Graham singled out a picture. He smiled tenderly at the memory.

"Leah looks even prettier there than she did at the senior prom."

"You talk as if she's old or something," Gwen chided. "That was only four years ago. You guys have been together for a long time. I'm surprised we aren't hearing wedding bells, brother dear."

"Not till Leah graduates and gets her career established."

"Not to mention yours," Gwen replied.

"I'm working on it. I told you at Christmas."

Dana flipped a page and picked up a loose snapshot. "Look at this one. At the beach. Your dad's riding both of you on his shoulders."

"That looks tricky," Graham commented, "but Dad was so

good at it. How old were we there? About three?"

Dana checked the back of the picture for a date. "Almost four," she said.

"Mom," Graham went on, "the way Dad's starting to forget everything, will he forget us too?"

"That can happen, honey, yes. But not for a long time."

Gwen slid over another page. "There's you and dad on your way to the Derby, Mom. You look like you're royalty. You're a princess in that fancy, wide-brimmed hat. What is it they say about our Derby? After the racehorses, it's the ladies' hats?"

Graham pointed to a picture and said, "There's Dad as the Grand Marshall at the Derby Parade. He sure was handsome. Still is."

"Look how distinguished Dad looks there with you in that picture, Mom," Gwen said, "at that charity ball. I wish he was here looking at these pictures with us."

Dana glanced up at her daughter, and Gwen said, "It hurts, what Dad did. But are we going to let it destroy our family?"

"No!" Dana replied, almost surprising herself at her enthusiasm. Almost. "We're a great family. Even though…your dad…even though…well…we need to hold on to *us*, don't we? All of us. Especially as your dad gets sicker."

Graham said, "You know, Mom, what Dad did…it doesn't diminish what we've always had. Who we are as a family. I mean, does it?'

"Illusions have certainly been shattered," Dana answered, "but this family, our love, that's precious. And you know something else? I think it's worth fighting for!"

* * *

Dana parked her SUV in the steep driveway at Claire's house

that night. She got out and climbed the steps. A lovely wreath of summer flowers decorated the front door. She rang the bell and waited, taking several deep breaths to calm her suddenly pounding heart. In a minute Claire opened the door and stared at her in surprise.

"You have something that belongs to me!" Dana announced.

And before Claire could react, she whipped past her and went inside. Claire closed the door and tagged along as Dana followed the TV sounds to the den at the end of the hall. Les lounged in one of a pair of recliners facing the TV armoire. He scooped popcorn from a bowl on his lap and watched an old courtroom movie classic titled "Absence of Malice" starring the late Paul Newman. Dana walked over and stopped between Les and the TV. Claire stopped behind her.

"Look who's here, Les. Dana just dropped in. Imagine that. Shall we tell her about our plans?" To Dana, she added, "Les was going to call you—"

"What plans?" Les asked Claire but he stared at Dana.

"You remember," Claire said. "My retirement. And your divorce."

Les looked astonished. "Dana, sweetheart, are we getting a divorce?"

"Over my dead body!" Dana cried. Then she smiled, softly. "Why don't you come back home with me instead?"

Les lowered the footrest on the chair and sat up. He placed the popcorn bowl on the side table. Claire looked alarmed and stepped around Dana and over to him.

"You don't want to leave, do you, Les?" Claire asked, placing a hand on his arm. "You want to stay here with me."

He stared at Claire, and then at Dana. His eyes went back to Claire. Returned to Dana. Claire. Dana. Claire. Dana. Time passed and he stared some more. At last, he stood. Claire stepped in his path, desperate, beseeching. She clutched his arm.

"No, Les, you don't want to leave. We've made all of our plans."

Suddenly, he looked bewildered. Then he shook free of her hold. "I…I think… I…I can't…I think…I'm…I'm supposed to go home with…with my wife."

CHAPTER 14

The June evening was warm and dry. On the Connelly's back lawn a volleyball game progressed on an open patch in the waning sunlight. Dana and Les on one team with two other male partners at Les's firm and their wives. Across the net Richard and his date played the game with two of the firm's paralegals and their significant others.

Later on the terrace, Les tended steaks and chicken on a big gas grill, while he and the other men nursed beers and talked politics. Dana and the other women arranged a buffet on a folding table outside the breakfast room, bringing out an assortment of side dishes that the ladies had made and brought over. They were catching up on the latest news and gossip when Les strode up to his wife.

"Sweetheart, did I tell you? The last baby in…in the blue jay family…the last baby left the…the nest this morning."

Dana smiled. "Yes, you told me, honey."

He nodded and started back to the grill. "I'm sure going to miss those little guys."

Gloria watched Les depart and said, "So, Dana, what did you think about Claire?"

Dana almost dropped the casserole dish that she carried. She recovered and sat it carefully down on the buffet. "What about her?" she asked.

"Les didn't mention it? I'm sure that Pete told him."

"Les probably forgot, Gloria."

"Oh. Right. Well, Claire gave the firm her notice two weeks ago. She put her house on the market and took off for the West Coast. Her brother lives out there."

Pete wandered over with his beer and took up the tale. "She'd been talking to some hot law firm out there. In San Diego. Some outfit that her brother does business with. Claire said they made her an offer she couldn't refuse."

"My woman's intuition tells me that there was more going on with Claire," Gloria said. "But who knows?"

"Dana," Pete said, "did Les tell you that he's going to start coming into the office a couple days a week and helping us out where he can? At least until we replace Claire."

"That will be so good for him, Pete," Dana replied. "He needs to feel useful. I don't have to tell you what a brilliant mind he had for the law."

"Your husband is the best trial lawyer I've ever seen," Pete said. "He cares—he *loves*—the law. And he's always fully committed to his clients."

Richard came over and joined them. "Since I live close, I can easily pick up Les for his days at the office."

Les walked over to his wife again. "Dana, sweetheart, did I tell you? The last blue jay baby left the nest."

"Yes, I know."

"How many times have I told you?"

"It's okay, honey."

"I'm sure going to miss those little guys."

* * *

In the garage the following morning, Les cleaned out the back of Dana's SUV. He reached in and moved an old blanket and discovered his toolbox. He slid it out, closed the door and sat the box on his workbench. He opened the lid. A few minutes later, tools spread around him, he held up a beautifully framed picture of his family taken at Gwen's college graduation. He studied it proudly and smiled.

That night in the master suite, Dana read a book in bed. Les entered from the hall with a blue patterned gift bag, white tissue paper poking out the top. He carried it to her bedside and she looked up. She scooted over so he could sit down. He presented his gift to her. She removed her reading glasses and laid them and her book on the night table.

"So what's the occasion?" she asked.

"Us. We're an occasion, don't you think?"

She smiled. "I do, yes."

She lifted the tissue paper out of the bag and reached in for her gift—a bronze-framed photo of Les and her with the twins at Gwen's college graduation ceremony.

"I'm sure proud of that picture," he said. "At least one of our kids finished college. And now she's in med school, right?"

"Yes…Thank you, Les, for the picture. Where did you get this frame? I don't think I've ever seen it before. It's lovely."

"I don't remember where it came from, but you'll never guess where I found the picture." He laughed softly. "I was cleaning out the back of your…your SUV—I think it was this morning—and I came across my toolbox. I went through it and found the picture. Shoved way back in there under the tools. I think…I think it's your gift that I forgot. How about that?"

"I'll treasure it, honey."

He kissed her cheek and headed for the adjoining bathroom.

She placed the picture on the night table.

"You should have a shower tonight, Les."

"I don't want a…a shower."

"Yes, please, Les." He groaned and she said again, "Please."

He groaned some more before agreeing. She went back to her book and the shower came on in the bathroom. Suddenly, she laid the book aside and grabbed the picture. She stared at it for a minute before flopping it over on her lap. She lifted off the backing and slipped out a picture behind the one of her family. She noted the date printed on the back—December 1996. She turned the photo over and stared at Les and Claire slow dancing at an office party. And she remembered.

* * *

At Les's retirement party last October at the Grand Oaks Country Club, Pete roamed among the guests snapping pictures. He made his way over to Dana and Les who were sipping drinks near the bar.

Pete said, "Les, I sure hate adding your retirement party pictures to the office album."

"How big is the album now, Pete?" Dana asked. "After almost thirty years?"

Claire and Richard came toward them and Pete said, "You'll have to ask Claire that one. She's our official keeper of the album."

* * *

Dana emerged from her memory and reattached the backing to the picture frame. She'd searched every nook and cranny in the house, and then in the garage, but she hadn't thought to check in Les's toolbox. Now, she recalled him putting it in the back of her SUV when they sold his Audi. She returned the photo to the bedside table and glanced toward the adjoining bath. The shower was still going. She slid out of bed with the picture of Les and Claire. Downstairs in the study, she flipped on the light switch and crossed to the shredder in the corner. She fed in the picture, and it was gobbled up with hardly a rumble. She smiled and brushed off her hands. So much for that.

She was in bed reading again when Les emerged from the bathroom and slid in next to her. She closed her book and laid it on the table with her glasses. She faced her husband and he started to reach for her. She spoke and he stopped in mid-hug.

"Les, a few weeks ago you left me and moved in with Claire. You remember doing that?"

He nodded warily. "I…I think so."

"Why did you do it? Can you remember?"

"I think…I think…because…because I thought you didn't want me anymore. When we got married, we vowed to forsake all others. Then I fell in love with Claire too and…and you can't forgive me."

She embraced her husband. "Yes, I can. I forgive you now. I do."

Les looked astonished. "How can you forgive me?"

"Because I love you."

They cuddled beneath the sheet and he said, "I love the way you smell, sweetheart. What is it when we go to bed?"

"My night cream."

"You're my night dream."

They kissed and he reached over her and shut off the lamp. Their family picture gleamed in the moonlight seeping in around the window treatments. Another kiss went from affectionate to passionate. Initiated by her.

"I think you want to fool around a little bit," he said.

"I want to fool around a whole lot."

He laughed softly. "I sure haven't forgotten how to do that."

Les cuddled his wife in a loving embrace. He kissed her ardently and slid down the strap of her gown over her shoulder. He pressed a kiss into her bare skin. And then another. And another.

THE END

Any errors in factual information regarding the disease of dementia are solely the fault of the author. Dementia is not merely an individual disease; it affects the entire family. If you or anyone you know is suffering through dementia, further information can be found by contacting the organizations below.

Alzheimer's Association: Alzheimer's Disease and Dementia
www.alz.org
800-272-3900

Dementia Society of America
PO Box 600, Doylestown, PA 18901
1-844-DEMENTIA (844-336-3684)
www.dementiasociety.org

The Association for Frontotemporal Degeneration (AFTD)
www.theaftd.org
267-514-7221
Toll-free HelpLine 866-507-7222

ABOUT THE AUTHOR

Dora Leigh has six prior novels to her credit, five inspirational romances and a mystery. The author's previously published books were written under her real name Dorothy Abel. *The Forgotten Gift* marks her return to full time writing after raising a family and working outside the home. In addition to being an active member of her church, she loves to read and take long walks outdoors. Leigh currently resides in Louisville, Kentucky.

CPSIA information can be obtained at www.ICGtesting.com
Printed in the USA
LVOW10s0409020615

440705LV00002B/4/P